#minithology

A MOST UNUSUAL GARDEN

EDITED BY N.D. GRAY

featuring

TRACY EIRE ELIZABETH KNOLLSTON N.D. GRAY

KARLI STITES HEIDI MOONE

CONTENTS

INTRODUCTION

OUR CONNECTION WITH GROWING THINGS is a sustaining connection. It draws many of us to attempt the seemingly impossible. Like growing a container garden in the middle of the Arizona heat—a vastly different experience from sowing seeds in the rich Ohio soil. My flowers have done well, but I'm uncertain I'll have any vegetables.

Our world is full of amazing and unique plants. The Talipot Palm which grows for eighty years. Blooms. And dies. The lithop which looks like living stones. Hoya Kerrii, a succulent with leaves that look like a heart.

Corpse Flower, Black Bat Flower, Ghost Orchid, Dragon's Blood Tree... the list of amazing, growing things goes on. All over the world, nature is full of more than just dandelions—which are, themselves, quite astounding and used to be planted on purpose. And our gardens display all these wondrous plants to which we are drawn.

For this #minithology, the contributors were invited to look beyond ordinary to the most unusual interpretation of "garden" our imaginations could create.

Inspired by fictional places such as the world of *Avatar*, the beauty of Rivendell, or the lovely gardens of L.M. Montgomery, and by the odd growths we have found in our own world—random wild flowers growing through cracks in the asphalt, skeleton flowers which become translucent when it rains, corn truffles, and the thirty thousand year old, viable seeds of an Arctic flower—each author has created a garden worth visiting.

These gardens are crossroads in our characters' lives, places where choices are made and lessons are learned. The tone of our stories slanted darker for this #minithology, but there is also sweetness and hope, like bright flowers among the deep, rich foliage.

Grab a sunhat and spade, a glass of iced tea, and join us in our most unusual gardens.

ND Gray
July 2021
Camp Verde, AZ

Tracy Eire connects more with wild and freely growing things as opposed to those cultivated in neat rows. As a child, she wandered the tundra and as an adult appreciates trees growing in places abandoned by humans. It is no surprise then that her favorite fictional garden-like space is Tolkien's Mirkwood.

Her story takes place in the wilds of game coding, where anything can grow if one can imagine it.

VOICE OF THE WILD

Tracy Eire

...SOON, WE'LL HAVE MUCH BETTER algorithms."

"Bruce, I swear you think you're paid by the word."

A crumpled candy-wrapper came out of the back of the office, bopped Terrel on the head, and rebounded onto the constellation Monoceros on the back of her hand. Which bumped Ada Keller back into the world again. She blinked her eyes in the here and now, no longer lost in the traffic, but seated at the desk in the slightly overheated open-office configuration, with her fan droning.

She seemed to wake up. "What are we talking about?"

Terrel was about 10 years older than Ada, and in charge of the offices that monitored the game fabric and network. He was thinning a bit at the top and greying at the temples. It had no effect on his vigor, or his looks. Bruce

Plaskett might manage the cold, cave-like server rooms, but in this neck of the woods Bruce could mess around all he wanted, it was Terrel Brown's turf.

Ada was glad about that. She'd *never* have worked for Bruce.

She glanced aside at her boss. He'd come down the hall and into this corner of his open space to scrutinize what Ada had been doing, not that she'd been aware. He did that a lot. And it wasn't weird, either. For his money—and there was currently a lot of money flowing through the seemingly ever-expanding office space of Triskele Monograph—Terrel stacked his chips on her. When things went wrong, Ada had the uncanny ability to right them again. "Never mind Bruce. Never mind any of them. Just tell me what you've got. What do you see?"

The guy beside her, Benedict, rolled his eyes. He didn't look at Ada, but it was possible for her to spot it in the edge of his phone screen. Ada couldn't *be* here, *everyone* had to have an opinion. Some disliked her *bitterly.* Benedict, who sat beside her, was considered her peer by everyone on the floor, and there was never any talk that suggested he was anything but her equal, not even from Terrel. It was fine if you could take being *equals* with a woman. Benedict couldn't.

Ada glanced at him, sidelong, "Find anything, Benedict?"

He went straight back to focusing on the data before him. He tended to be lazy.

She scrolled into her notes and slid them on the screen closest Terrel. "This. I found this."

"Terrific." Terrel rubbed his hands together. "What is this?"

Even Benedict scanned her monitor, and he started assembling a report based on her query, "I think... she found a—"

Ada ignored this, "I keep spotting an instance of the game code over-writing Co-op-ID when the users' game clocks exceed 24 hours in difference. You can change the game clock, which means that it seems like it's random at first. It's not, or I don't think it is. The ID reset is a quick, but easy to test." She opened a hand at the logs.

The aircon clicked in at last above her head, and Ada feared that she might be sweaty with so many people around her. But if she was, Terrel officially didn't care. He leaned in and squinted at it. "How did you even *see* that?"

"Uh. Tools. Queries. Like there's a," she glanced at him, "game in the game."

"An in-game game." He followed this.

"Right. And it's only active during game night. I saw a lot of clock resets, and occasionally there would be this call to refresh a token that has the Co-op-ID in it. It's like the code gets confused about which clock is getting reset—the game's, or the computer's? Could be a mistaken value somewhere in the code?" She tucked everything into a share that led to Terrel's desktop, thought about popcorn for lunch, and mailed him the explanation she'd been writing up.

Ada's data wasn't pretty. But it was *right*.

Benedict could have helped with that.

If he hadn't been a complete snake.

When she glanced, Mimi stood with her arms crossed behind them both. If you were going to have backup, you couldn't have done better than Mimi Alexandria. Ada felt more secure with the other girl hovering there.

"Outstanding. Outstanding, Ada." Terrel clapped the rounded padding at the top of her chair in glee. "I'll mail the findings to the head office and see what they have to say about it. Excellent work."

"Okay." She said as he headed for the door. "Can we talk about my shift sometime?"

He paused at the door with Bruce. "I need your skills on the graveyard, Ada. There's no one else with your chops working those hours. Nothing about that has changed."

Ada's face fell, and she knew it did, as much as she tried not to betray her disappointment. For one thing, it wasn't welcome in a corporate setting. For another, it would give Benedict and his bloodsuckers ammunition to hurl against her sore points later, and she couldn't be seen to have soft spots here. She nodded and went back to her computers.

Mimi turned and sped out after their boss without a word.

Maybe she couldn't stand to see her friend shot down.

And maybe it burned her not to be able to offer some coffee and comfort. That sounded like Mimi. The young women had an entirely different set of rules in the office than the guys.

Benedict bumped her chair. "You found the bug. *You* babysit it. We're going to lunch."

The aircon cooled the room enough that she could reach out and switch off her fans. Ada had lots of fans. She couldn't catch a break.

ADA'S SHIFT WAS ON HER mind as she trudged to the bus through the rain and rode home in the pong of wet Melton cloth. She had. A terrible. Shift. And as she'd asked for better it had slowly twisted into something worse and worse.

She'd wanted some day shifts.

And that's what she'd gotten.

Outside the bus windows—she was a stander in standing room only—the neighbourhoods started going a little to pot, a *little* downhill in the pouring rain. Lightning wove through the clouds overhead, and she wasn't the only one to duck down and peek out at the flash. Several seconds later thunder bumbled after it, the clumsy twin, upending a shelf full of knickknacks to the floor of the heavens. She was like that.

Her best efforts had ended in her having a day shift Monday and Tuesday, which started at 10 AM and ran for 6 hours each day, and overnight shifts that started at 7 PM for the rest of the week. The net result was a confused sleep schedule with some stomach sickness that she had a reasonable expectation was about to get much worse.

The bus hissed at the sidewalk to help a wheelchair board. It was packed in here, but people shuffled out of the way to help the man in the chair get to a place. It was a decent crowd on the bus home. Every one of them was too bushed to be an a-hole, no matter what the day had held.

She got off three stops from there, in the treed neighbourhood of her parent's house. She trotted through puddling and up the steps on the way to check her mother. Ada's mom had broken her foot in some exercise related enterprise or other. Ada clucked her tongue at finding the front door unlocked, stepped into a chaos of shoes, and shut and barred the door behind her.

"Hi Sunshine." Her dad said from the front room where he was putting together a camera tripod in front of an exercise bike. "Dom's here with the kids already."

She stared at the small sea of UGGs. "Yep." Dom was her oldest brother. He and his wife Cherry had 4 girls and a boy. It made her wonder if she was really needed here if this many people had descended on her mom. She set down her backpack stepped out of her Wellies and walked in to help her father with the tripod and wiring for the video camera.

Her mother was something of an exercise maven on YouTube.

No surprise that Ada was the one to add the camera to the network.

"Sure glad you came along when you did." Her father said cheerfully.

"You don't need me for this," Ada laughed at the notion. "You put together airplanes."

Her father wagged a finger at her. "My work has nothing to do with Wi-Fi networks. You're a wonder with Wi-Fi networks. You're better than Apple geniuses."

Ada laughed at that.

"You're wasted on that gaming company," her father told her.

"I *wish*," Ada laughed, a little embarrassed. "I don't even work at the gaming company. I work for a company that works for *them*."

She smoothed her blouse and stepped back to the camera to flick it on. Then she went to the nearby desktop to confirm that it was capturing the bike against her mother's green screen. Her father poked on frame to wave and strike a few poses. Ada laughed at him, but she made sure to save the footage onto the hard drive. She even popped in one of the USB drives on her keychain to take a copy for herself. Her dad was a complete ham, and in the very best sense of the word.

Ada missed the noise level rising, but glanced to find her mother, crutch under one arm, ambling into the front room.

She waved back at Cherry, who headed for the kitchen in the back of the house. Dom's girls tumbled and washed against the front door's supply of identical UGGs, and rushed outside with a golden retriever puppy following them. The youngest kid was still too small to head out on his own and was probably sleeping in the kitchen with his mother.

Ada glanced aside at her mother settling into a chair with Dom's help. "You got them a puppy?"

"It's supposed to be for Donnie," Dom told her. "He plays with it, but he's still a bit too small. It'll work out."

"*It'll work out*, all right," Ada grinned. "Those girls already love that puppy!"

Her mother's head rose sharply, trim, toned, and lightly wrinkled. She scanned what Ada was wearing and frowned. "Have you gained weight?"

"Uh, a little." Ada said. "There's a lot of stress at work."

Her mother waved a hand in air. "Your father will bring you a folding bike." Because Ada's mother had exercise equipment from her sponsors and was always outfitting her children. Ada nodded at the notion though.

"I appreciate it, Mom. And, excellent news, your new camera's working." She shut the thing off and took the connecting cable from her father to get its battery charging. "What happened to your foot?"

"I dropped a weight." She sighed and smoothed a toned calf. "You like the dog? We're still trying to name it."

"Uh, what about Turing?" Ada noted.

Her mother rolled her eyes, "For heaven's sake, nothing geeky. It's bad enough you're not married yet because of those hours you keep. You're not even *engaged*. What happened to that boy, Tom, you were seeing?"

She inspected the thumb drive she closed into her pocket. "We had a fight, Mom. I told you. He took his stuff and left. He's not coming back."

"That's because *you* couldn't *begin* to compromise." Her mother threw up her hands. "I have no idea what's wrong with you."

Dom came out of the kitchen and set a drink down in front of her mother. "She's got a point."

Ada's dark eyes darted up, "It's not *compromise* when only one person has to do it."

"You're too picky, too invested in that stupid gaming company." The woman complained.

"I don't work at a–" Ada shook her bobbed hair. "*So*, you got the camera I recommended, right? Did you get to shoot any test footage with it?"

"*I* did," her father interjected. "If anyone wants to see it, Ada can do that thing she does where she puts what's on the laptop on the television screen?"

But it didn't work.

Her mother kept on, "You should have been able to hold on to Tom. He was a nice boy. That would have worked out if you were ever as serious about your relationships as you were about making money for your boss."

Dom laughed on the end of that, "You should date *him*."

Ada froze at the words. So casual. So *stupid*. She honestly thought it would take a guy like her older brother, Dom—blissfully unaware of the lives of others—to blurt out something so sexist without a single thought to how difficult it was for women in some workplaces.

As politely as she could, Ada said, "Oh, I don't know, Dom, why didn't you date *Grace*. She's your administrative assistant, right?"

He was suddenly offended. Apparently, what was good for the goose was not, in fact, good for the gander. The gander had extra-special thin skin.

"It's no different for me," Ada told him.

"It was a joke." Dom said sharply. "And you had to be *insulting*."

"When you say the same thing, it's *funny*, am I right?" Ada smiled across at him. She wasn't in the mood, she realized, not for any of it. "I'm only here to make sure Mom is okay."

"Oh, *I* seem to be an afterthought in all this." Ada's mother pushed her blonde dye-job up into a tail and tied it off with a scrunchy. "Never mind me. I'm the one with the *injury*. And who is *gifting* you an exercise bike. Why consider my feelings?"

Ada held her temper and exhaled through her mouth. She had too much to say to speak.

"Honey, Ada's come right from work," Ada's father noted. "She's had a long day."

"Yes. Yes. That's true." Ada's mother shifted in the massage recliner she'd gotten from a company called Brookbane last year, during her *'Right Body? Beach Ready!'* series. Now she collapsed back against it like the victim Ada was sure she *was* in her own story. "That's the reason she can't hold on to a man like Tom. So, no grandchildren for me."

"*You have 5.*" Ada snapped.

"What's the point of bringing life into the world when it gives as little back as you do, Ada? I ask you." The woman threw up her hands. "A husband *is* a job. A family *is* a job. What's a gaming company compared to a family? *Shame* on you."

Yet, she didn't see Dom unemployed. Ada shook her head and backed away.

"Honey, wait a second." Her father tried. "Your mother's painkillers—"

"Dad, you don't have to spin a wheel for me." Ada headed back toward her boots and bag.

"What's that supposed to mean?" Her mother shouted at her.

Ada poked her head around the hall again to say, "It means you have enough excuses to put on the Wheel of Fortune for the Final Spin, Mom." She nodded before she tucked a foot in her rain boot and caught up the other. *Chew on that.*

"You're a terrible person to say something like that to your long-suffering mother!"

"Oh, you *always* make sure we suffer back," Ada grumbled before she caught up her bag and found her father standing in the hallway, distressed, and kind of helpless. She sucked in a deep breath and nodded. "It was nice to see you, Dad, and do some work with you."

"Yeah. I love you, honey."

"Me too." She checked her watch, "I've gotta go if I'm going to make the bus."

"You go on, honey." He nodded at her and eyed the sky, which, though no longer raining, was threatening. "I'd better get the girls in. Uh, and I like *Turing.* It's distinguished."

She smiled back at him before she headed down the steps. "Thanks, Dad."

But it didn't shut out her mother's angry bellowing from the front room, "Ada, you don't have a maternal bone in your body! Everything I passed on to you shriveled up long ago!"

Heading across the garden full of wet grass, girls, and frolicking puppy, Ada heard herself think the bitter words 'My God, I hope so'.

ON WEDNESDAY, THE BUS DROPPED her off at Triskele Monograph at 5:55 PM.

She was almost late when she arrived at her desk and Benedict bumped up against her shoulder. "Lots of luck with tonight. And *every night-shift after*, Ada."

The guy who sat across from her hid his mirth badly as he got up to leave with Benedict.

Ada swept the crumbs out of her chair and ignored them.

As the sound of the elevator they took to the ground floor died, she felt the skin of her eyelids prick and had to fight to keep her lips from crumpling together. She reminded herself that she was lucky to be here. That she was valuable. And she was doing what made her happiest. But it was still hard.

The scent of nachos drew in on her before she was aware of it.

Someone set down a pair of soft drinks with a clack and intoned. "Do you believe that he and Dougie stayed late to do that? I mean, what kind of *losers*?"

Wide-eyed, Ada turned and straightened to find Mimi. "Oh, my gosh. What are you doing here?"

"I'm getting us cheesy nachos." She lifted the loaded tray she held.

"I, uh." She took the tray, which was more than enough for two people, and set it down on the desk between their stations.

Mimi said nothing else. She pulled a squirt bottle of sour cream out of one pocket of her apron and set it on the desk. Then she opened the tins of pop. "So... I ran after Terrel and asked to go on the split shift with you. He's been looking for someone to back you up after all."

"Why?" Ada's world flipped. She was suddenly happy, almost over-joyed, with the split shift. But her astonishment made her words forceful. "*Why* would you *do that*?"

"Well, for one, I want to learn from you. And two," she paused here for a moment to think through what she was going to say next. "We've got to stick together. So. What do you say? Teach me?"

Ada chuckled and wiped her face with a sleeve. "You got it."

"He's trying to beat you." Mimi sat down and stared at Benedict's setup. "But he really needs to be trying to beat *us*. Right now, he's better than I am. Maybe it'll stay that way, but, I guess, not without a fight."

"I'll help you in any way I can." Ada grinned as the girl passed her and turned her screens to face them both. She also pulled her chair over. "What are we doing tonight?"

"Uh," Ada picked up and moved her drink. "How about you study my screens and we start to talk about how things look when they're normal."

"Eat some nachos." Mimi gave the plate a little shove. "Or I'll eat them all. And what are you talking about 'normal'?"

"It's like life. If you can't tell how it should be, you won't recognize when it isn't right." Ada couldn't stop smiling. Every time she touched her keys, energy ran through her fingertips. Mimi had always been insightful and always been fun. She was accomplished at diffusing. The thought of having an ally in the middle of all this? It had the same head-buzzing effect as a full cup of wine.

"And *then* he started to reverse engineer what you did on the screen. But he didn't see that I'd come in an hour early—I mean these nachos don't make themselves." Mimi rolled her almond-shaped dark eyes. "So, I watched him and Dougie trying to figure out how you did it."

"Yeah?" Ada's teeth bared. "Let me show you."

"Wait. Show me the screens and let's see if anything pops for me," Mimi said.

Ada brought them all up, rolled her chair back, and grabbed the nacho chips. "How long do you want to go at this?"

"How long did it take you?" Mimi asked.

Good question. "To notice it? I saw it right away. To figure out the rest? Hours."

They passed most weeks honing one another's skills. A person couldn't teach without being taught. Not 1 to 1 anyway. There were tools that Mimi knew better, and she taught them to Ada. And Ada knew the logs so well that a small wobble in the network traffic could wake her from highway hypnosis. Speaking of which... they were also practiced at keeping one another awake.

The nights had patterns. Ada would come yawning from a nap on the couch of a manager's office and Mimi would have her feet kicked up and wave her in. Or Mimi would crash and wake to Ada frantically typing and sending logs to the gaming company, fresh out of her tools. And she'd point at Mimi's monitors. And at breakfast. Mostly, they'd sit back and understand things about a game neither of them had really played.

The evening that Ada showed up a half an hour early, she found Mimi setting down her bags and talking to Benedict.

"What's it called?" Mimi popped a bubble.

"Voice of the Wild." Benedict tapped his keyboard and scoffed. "How do you not *get* that and still work here?"

"Because I didn't," Mimi replied. "I'm still capable of doing my job."

"Says you." Benedict pulled up the online game on his largest screen. "*This… is it.*"

Pearly clouds of white, lilac, and orange painted across a convex blue sky. Complex architecture built out of lights that arched through air. Music rose as a round, silvery-wood door came together in the middle of the sky, and railings and stairs fell out of it toward the player. It was so lovely it might have inhabited some elven domain—some fairyland—invisible to mankind. Benedict logged in. "I'm a level 60 with 5 of my 10 characters in here. A *fire-breathing badass*, and you've never even seen the home screen."

"Hopeless," Dougie confirmed from where he observed the goings on. "You can build out this world too, using the CraftEngine. I have like… 8 Dwellings, and my own Realm now? Not that you'd understand what *that* means."

Benedict turned aside to Mimi, "Trust me, *it's hard.* But… I doubt Dougie is like some of the losers on this platform, *100% there to Build a Bear.*"

Both the guys laughed, and finger-shot at one another.

"Voice has been out there for 2 and a half years now." Dougie nodded at the screen. "Some gamers, right? They've never killed a troll, never thrown a rock—"

"*Never kicked a stick.*" Benedict said the words as if it was Official Lingo. And they both laughed at that for a moment.

Then Dougie continued, "All they've done, for 2-point-5 years is build Realms. There are the guys who make massive, sprawling, realms you can free-play in, like *Behemoth, Pound-sand, Thunderous-Wonderous,* and *Mother May I,* that are like, easily 100 Realms sewn together. There are about 10,000 super-vast ones. There's a smaller list of something like 100 private, invitation-only, Locked-Door Realms. Like," he hunted around in a desk mate's paper pile until he found a list he shoved at Mimi, "haven't you seen this?"

Mimi took the paper and read a few of the names from the top. "Uhm, *28 Days, Floodgates of Avalon, Dutch Apples,* uh–"

Benedict snatched the paper, which he crumpled and tossed in his bin. "First, that's Vinnie's stuff. Second, ignore the Locked-Door Realms, Mims. The reason there are so few of them is only complete losers pour that much time into a build and never let anyone else play its levels." He got to his feet and locked his machine. "Catch you losers later. Have fun in the night-shift ghetto."

"What'd he just say?" Mimi turned to Ada as the two young men left.

Ada pulled the crumpled paper out of the garbage bucket and aped Benedict, "*Firstly, that's Vinnie's stuff, but I'm okay to crush it and throw it away.*" She set to unfolding it and set it under network manuals to flatten as much as it could.

"Paper's never the same." Mimi said with a windy sigh.

Ada smiled at the other girl's attitude. "Ain't it the truth."

"So, you're telling me they spent all this money on this game and only guys play it?" Mimi shook her head at the logging that rolled by on her own monitor.

"Not true. Women are 40% of the gaming market and growing." Ada grinned, "And what do you think *28 Days* indicates? Or *Mother May I?*"

Mimi seemed to have a little more hope and life about *Voice of the Wild* after that. They settled in on what should have been a pretty normal evening and overnight.

"I mean it looks sharp." Mimi gestured at the screen. "We should play it."

"Uh. I mean, if you logged in right now, that would let me record the normal process for login and build out in the North American servers, end-to-end. I don't know if you've ever seen it. But it's a huge process, signing up, dropping the base world, and the random selector for the first free characters. It's got a lot of moving parts to get down, and I've found lots of bugs there." She turned to Mimi and found her on the sign-up page.

"Nope." She nipped her lip and burst into an excited smile. "But can you get a capture ready if I'll use my Triskele login?"

"That'll be easy for me to trap." Ada tapped through narrowing her logging. It was possible to do a manual trace, not just rely on the Machine Learning. She coordinated with Mimi so the automated playbook she needed running was alive and kicking by the time the creation of her profile went through.

The playbook recorded everything that branched out from that event, and both girls huddled to inspect it. "That's new," Ada noted. They had pulled out popcorn for this and muttered as the screens clicked up and data rolled out.

But the sudden flicker of red on Ada's right made both the girls turn.

And stay that way.

It remained red.

"What's that," Mimi huffed with amusement, "Your conditional formatted screen has lost its mind, girl."

Ada hopped up from her chair and went to the hefty monitor hanging on the wall to their right. She picked out her own screen and double-tapped it to bring up the display. Mimi joined her.

"What is it... are we being... hacked or something?" She slowed the scroll on her own screen by half. "Damn, this is a shit-tonne of data. This is, like, choke the pipe, stop the presses, Hoover-dam busted, kinda–"

"It locks the backups." Ada dropped the channel changer, turned in place and ran for her desk. "It-locks-the-backups-it-locks-the-backups!" As quickly as her quivering fingers could while watching the cascading delete, she logged into the game servers, got temporary access, and copied one backup, *without* pasting it.

"Whoa. Whoa, Ada," Mimi straightened. "This is.... This is *user-initiated*."

"That much data?" Ada gestured at the screen. "This delete is still running and it's been over 5 minutes, Mimi." She stood there, unsure what to do, as the log beside her rolled on in red. It seemed to take half an hour. But only 10 minutes passed between someone, somewhere in the world pressing Delete, and the final disposal checks to run.

Then it was done.

All the backups were locked down and were marked for deletion too.

Except... for the ephemeral copy she had taken, from the morning.

And Ada hadn't clicked *Paste* yet.

She stared at the logging as it stopped scrolling red.

"What did we lose?" Ada asked Mimi.

"I'm not sure." Mimi told her and shook her head. "This is a lot of data to process if we want to find out and I'm kinda busy being *mind-blown* right now."

They both stood in silence for a moment.

Then Ada's desk phone rang.

She picked it up with her left hand without thinking. "Yep?"

"Ada, it's Dougie." He added onto the end, "Don't hang up."

She eyed the phone she held to her ear. Because he knew she was well within her rights to. "Why not? I'm busy."

"I... I bet you are." Somewhere in the room behind him, heat kicked in, and a cat mewed.

He had a cat.

Dougie said, "I'm gonna send you a website–"

"Send it to Mimi." Ada shook her head.

"Okay. It's on the way to both of you, uh...."

She could hear him tapping keys and clicking his mouse.

"Talk, or I'm going to hang up," Ada told him.

Mimi leaned in to reflect, "Dougie sent me to a post on *Voice of the Wild's* core message board, and the topic is, I kid you not. *WTF-happened?*"

"What's going on?" She asked either of them.

"Uh... one of the locked-worlds unlocked about a half an hour ago. So, we all piled in. There had to be thousands of people in seconds just... running in across bridges. It's gorgeous. Sun, fields of flowers of every kind in the game ... there were elk and boar and... butterflies. I got to see the World Banner. Then it was gone."

Ada peeked across at the cursor in the back-up server. "World?"

"Yep," Dougie told her. "I respawned in my own Realm again. *Boom*. I tried to go back. A lot of people did. But the messaging system kept reading *deleting-deleting*, until it was gone. *Deleted*."

"Yeah, we saw a *massive* data dump on this end. What was the world name?" Ada asked.

"It was *Breath of Life*," he told her.

"Okay, hang on." Ada edged by her chair and pushed the books off the sheet of paper on Vinnie's desk. It was doing a little better than it had been earlier. She scanned the list.

1. 28 Days
2. Floodgates of Avalon
3. Dutch Apples
4. サクランボ
5. 火災
6. Blue Door
7. Watashi no tochuu de
8. **Breath of Life**

"Tell me if you see anything?" Dougie asked her.

Mimi straightened and made wide-eyes. "Ada, the forums are *absolutely on fire*. Apparently, when a large 'world' opens up, you hear these trumpets in-game, and there's confetti over this star on the map screen, and you can teleport right to it." She spun the screen. "Servers fell down and couldn't get up, so many people teleported into this place."

She pushed an ID across the desk at Ada.

Ada, in turn, gawped up at the ghostly backup folder on the side of her home screen.

The IDs checked out.

"Dougie-I-gotta-go." She hung up the line and stood straight to stare down at the paper. According to it, *Breath of Life* was the 8th biggest private Realm in the game. Mimi kept reading comments aloud on her right. This kept up until Ada had to throttle the message board servers and automatically create a backup to share the load.

"I see what you did there." Mimi nodded at the backup. "You know you gotta dump the ephemeral copy. If it's even complete. Customer decides to nuke one of the most stacked worlds in the game? None of our business."

"But *why*?" Ada asked.

"I dunno. Because they accidentally opened it up to everyone else and... freaked out?" Mimi turned back to her message boards. "But it's your *job* if you paste that. Not that it matters. Your admin privileges will run out in 10 minutes anyway."

Yeah. Ada eyed the timer at the bottom of her screen. *They would.*

She scrolled down to the Hold folder, clicked in, and made a folder called Arbitration.

Then she right clicked the mouse... and pasted.

The volatile data started quietly unloading into the folder.

See, Mom? It's not only my boyfriend. I'm gonna lose my job.

Mimi started to read aloud, and Ada wasn't sure if her friend was wrapped up in the threaded conversations, or if it was a smokescreen between herself and whatever Ada had chosen to do.

It was the news of the night, and that kept Mimi and Ada occupied long after the paste completed.

A FULL 2 WEEKS LATER, Ada lay on her bed on her day off, still employed. No one had even noticed. *Breath of Life* sat in Arbitration, unmolested.

She'd waited until the *official dump date*, after which nothing could be restored, and no Un-delete Request came. Ada didn't understand. The massive properties didn't... vanish.

By now she'd done the research. She flipped pages to peruse her notes.

> *June of last year the owner of How Do U Like Them Apples returned to the server for the first time in 4 months. Turned over the key codes to the Realm to Little Dutch Diva, who did a RealmMerge() that took 2 months to complete –– Dutch Apples. [Rumored private transaction]*
>
> *January 6th the owners of #16 Wrath and Ruin made the Realm public.*
>
> *March 10th, consolidation of Wrath and Ruin with Angel Gate –– Wrath Angel Ruin Gate (#12)*

Ada rolled across her comforter and picked at the edge of the journal because, in her guts, she knew something was wrong here. Realms that large were worth money. When they were built out like *Dutch Apples*, or *Wrath and Ruin*, they could be shown like a luxury car and *sold*.

What had happened?

And why had she kept the backup?

It... hadn't been for her sake.

Even if she now knew it was worth a mound of dough.

She didn't want to sell it—didn't want it *at all*.

Ada wasn't a gamer.

And what she'd done was illegal. *Completely* illegal. Which was currently *killing her softly*.

She'd get fired at Triskele Monograph and sued by *Voice of the Wild* if anyone found out.

"This is... ridiculous." She shut the book and laid it on her belly. "I have to do something."

In fact, she got up and paced to her window that Saturday morning, she'd been thinking about this for days, and... she had the information she needed now. She smoothed her jeans and went through the small apartment looking for her slip-on runners. Where had she left them?

Her message light blinked by the phone and she tapped it on the way by.

The machine said, "Ada, this is your mom. Call me back, okay, honey?"

Ada steeled herself and said, "No." Especially not with what she'd done now. Her mother would have a field day if nerves hit, and Ada let that slip. And she'd deserve it. She still didn't even understand why she'd done this. Ada continued to her backpack, took out the cell phone she'd bought at a pawn shop, and turned into a burner.

Then she went out back of her apartment building for a walk. It was mostly parkland there, and quiet. She walked all the way down to the lake on the other side, sat at a bench, and sent a message.

She took out the notebook and found the number she needed.

Then she texted.

What happened with Breath of Life?

The text stayed that way through shopping for vinyl records, a jog, a second shower, Korean barbeque, and a bookstore. She was back in her apartment peeling boiled eggs when the burner made a bleat at her. She wasn't used to the sound, so it made her jump.

Ada wetted and wiped her hands before she went to check her text messages. The reply was:

Who are you?

Well, that was an solid question. Ada remembered her plate of boiled eggs and asparagus spears and carried it and the phone to her cup on the 2-person table. She set the burner out beside her and typed:

Just tell me what happened.

There was a delay. It was almost midnight, and she was in bed, drifting, when the phone bleated in her kitchen. She gathered herself and padded out in her underwear and sleep tee. The reply text said:

It wasn't my fault.

Ada was still thinking about that response while she was tracking anomalies in the game the next day. She got to her feet about halfway through the day and decided to leave for the afternoon. This meant she had to drop by Terrel's office, where he was on the phone.

Mentally, she wasn't able to do what she loved to do.

Worst thing was, she'd done this to herself.

Her boss muted the phone, "What's up Ada?"

"I have to go." She told him with a nod.

"I thought you were pale." He set down his headset and stood up. "Something I can do?"

"I'll work extra hours," she told him.

"No-no. Go," he told her. "Go home and rest."

She trudged back to her seat to collect her stuff.

"You okay?" Mimi frowned up at her.

"Something I have to take care of."

"Well okay, because you look like death."

Ada checked her locked machines and was still chuckling at that on the way to the elevator. She went out onto the street and bypassed the bus stop as she walked. She typed and sent:

'It wasn't my fault?' What does that mean?

But there was no answer. She stopped in a coffee shop and waited, but it didn't make a difference. Her nerves were too on edge to endure waiting.

"I'm sorry... but it's time for the big guns." Ada took out her laptop and remoted into her desktop at work. She had the phone number. It took her about 10 minutes to work her way to the billing address. Once she had it and dropped the connection, she packed up and left.

She felt desperate walking the streets, thinking, *What the hell am I doing?*

What did she want from this person?

By the time darkness fell and she paced the floor of her 1000 square feet, the rattling of her nerves met the boiling in her mind to create a symphony of worries. Finally, she gave in and threw her hands up.

Ada made her way into what the floor plans for this place called a 'den'—6x7 feet right off the hall from the front door. As she stood in the doorway, the wall to her right separated her apartment from the outside hall, and there were no windows, but it wasn't... *bad*. Still stank of fresh paint. Maybe it was taking a while to dry because it was enclosed? She crossed the drop sheet and checked the vents. Then she considered the wall that was, essentially, the outside hall. It wasn't loud in this building. The walls were well insulated, thankfully.

Ada took the air purifier out of its box and got it working in the kitchen.

No need to expose herself to fumes.

Then she installed it.

"Maybe it'll take some of the paint scent out of the air?" She shrugged.

The bleat of the phone in the kitchen brought her out again.

She shut the door behind her, air purifier humming quietly in her silent apartment.

A Most Unusual Garden

Ada took the phone to her laptop in the kitchen before she settled down and remoted in at work. Then she spun up a *huge* test environment. And checked the clock. It was 9:30 in the evening when she did the unthinkable. She installed and spun up *Breath of Life.*

She logged into the game as a test user and slid on her virtual reality glasses.

The clouds peeled back around her, and the great round door rose up.

Was *Breath of Life* worth saving?

She paused only to get her wireless laptop controller.

Then she sat down and... clicked through the door.

The first thing she saw, and she wasn't very sharp with the controller, so it was difficult, was a covered timber-trussed bridge. It was red and long and it was shadowy. The opposite side of the game was a pall of horror-movie like darkness.

"Okay. Little Silent Hill. But okay." Ada pushed down on the urge to logout. She had her fill of feeling overwhelmed in her life all ready, and enough private fears to pack a bus full of gremlins. But... she pressed on because the question wasn't answered yet.

Was it worth saving?

The way across the covered bridge was dark, and she could hear wind against the walls and eaves of this place. The staggered windows threw down squares of watery light as she walked, but she carried on, even though she didn't know what to expect. Inside her head, she heard Dougie's voice, talking about the elk and boar.

That didn't stop her worrying that, any moment, something would pop out at her from the gloom ahead. Ada steeled her nerves, picked up speed, and thumped against the wall. The... she wasn't used to the controls and forgave herself. Righted, Ada ran for the other side of the bridge, and as she picked up speed, the darkness began to peel back, and she made out... shapes.

The shapes had... limbs. She had to squint.

She turned up the sound for help but that gave her little more than howling wind.

At first.

The sweeping shapes resolved together, and by the time she *really* made them out it was too late. The Aspen trees lifted their limbs in a rush of green, light, and rising music, and, because she was going so fast, she ploughed out through the tips of their fingers and hurtled into space. Leaves brushed out behind her, and she launched over the edge of a massive fault-line. She'd run off a cliff. Birds spilled from the shrubs and growing things on the side of that mountainous drop. Far below her, wild horses tore aside through waving grasslands so high they rolled like an ocean. Golden motes of pollen whirled around their bodies, and everything—wildflowers, flying manes, leaves— everything pulsed with the wind. Music built up around Ada.

The sky above her unfurled a blowing yellow banner over the scudding clouds. It read:

Breath ~ of ~ Life

Ada clapped a hand to her mouth and swept off her headset.

What the...!

For a moment she sat with the custom music spinning through her apartment and her. It poked in between her cells, hopeful. Determined. Filled with courage. She stared from one side to the other in the dimness of her kitchen.

"No." She shook her head. Finally, she collected herself enough to slide the glasses back into place and turn on her Game Camera. She clicked record.

The paused session still had the banner unfurling.

As she hung in the wind, golden light, and tumbling swallows, she saw it flag.

Breath ~ of ~ Life

By: FallenStarscape
Realm champion: FallenStarscape

She got a glimpse of that before she plummeted.

But then the Realm did the most amazing thing. Something she knew the automation could do, if you learned how to use the game-code well, but... she'd never seen it used like this before. While she dropped like a stone, the wind swept her—by the compass rose in the game—due West, and the land flexed East. She plunged into the deep belly of a waterfall-fed pool. The water was *so mild and clear* in the sun, she spotted the ladder legs that led up again.

Ada's character rose in an arc through water filled with frilled and waving fronds and neon seahorses. It was like she was a cork. She caught the ladder and climbed out onto stones. There, the grass and wildflowers blew, and bees... a carpet of bees. A magic carpet of bees.

When Ada took off the headset this time, she also reached out and touched the screen to stop and send the recording. Then she got up and paced.

Finally, she took a deep breath, snatched up the phone, and scrolled to the latest text, because, so help her, if this person was about to tell her to flush that Realm...! But the text said:

It <u>wasn't me</u>.

Ada laid down the phone while staring at the wall. That gut instinct inside her had been... dead right. Here she'd been, brain churning, trying to work out how she could convince this user to reinstate and then either sell, or open this world. And the user *hadn't* triggered the delete.

Which meant someone else had.

The phone startled her when it buzzed. The text said:

Are you there?

She nipped the edge of her lip and replied.

Tell me your username in Voice.

The reply came:

FallenStarscape. I built Breath of Life.

"Whacha gonna do now, dammit Ada?" She pushed a hand back

through her hair and paced the kitchen. Somewhere in revolutions that took her through her living and dining room and back to her kitchen again, she decided herself.

I'm A-Da. Don't bother looking for me in-game. You won't find me. But I want to talk to you about Breath of Life. I know you live in New York City. Where's good?

She didn't get a reply that night. Which was fine. She'd expected this to go slowly once she'd made it weird. To her, it made perfect sense that she could have information like this. But to whomever the heck—she checked the wad of print-out she'd smuggled out with her this morning—whoever this guy was, she was doing a killer stalker impression about now.

"Oh my God, you're exactly the *weirdo* your mother says you are," She told herself on her way to her washroom.

She had to run a bath and think.

THE CONVERSATION WENT DARK FOR days.

Ada sat with Mimi, slurping Ramen noodles in front of a massive network trace when she got another response. She almost missed it in the noise of eating supper while Voice of the Wild was running a humongous update.

"*Ooh* they're all locked out of the game right now. *Ooh*, they're pacing the floor, tearing stuff apart with their teeth, freaking out," Mimi said. She was a player now and often in the forums.

Ada chuckled. "Only 15 more minutes... *if* it keeps going like this."

Mimi gestured at the screen, "Smooth."

"Like butter." Ada reached to check her phone.

Saturday.

And *FallenStarscape* sent a map with a dot on it, and a time scrawled beside it.

"You've been checking that phone like a man cheating." Mimi chuckled and her eyes widened. "Wait a sec? Am I sensing boyfriend vibes here?"

"*Nothing* like that." Ada laughed the thought off.

While they continued to watch the Cloud server logs rolling in, Ada was quietly worried. Now she was in the position of going somewhere unfamiliar, to meet a total stranger. Not her best move. She was kicking herself that she hadn't chosen some nearby police station.

But it was done now.

Done badly.

But done.

SATURDAY MORNING, ADA ROLLED OUT of bed, ran to the bathroom, and mostly puked in the toilet. Her nerves were a little fried. That never helped her aim.

It didn't help that she'd slept in.

She had to be quick getting ready to go.

Her machine was blinking, and she tapped it on the way to the door to put on shoes.

The message rolled: "Ada, It's Mom. I've given you days. It is high time you apologize! What kind of daughter makes her own mother wait like this? You act so much like a child that I sometimes can't believe you're a young woman and–"

She shut and locked the door on the rest of it, and then hurried down the hall.

Something about that was freeing. She felt a little lift inside, like running off the covered bridge, through the trees, and hanging in the sundrenched air. That had been kinda cool.

The elevator made a ping on her floor behind her, but she was already smiling on her way down the stairs by the time her mother came to fume and rage-hammer her front door. For whole minutes.

Ada and her father, sitting in the minivan, missed one another too.

And so, that morning, Ada went on her fateful way in the sunshine, and made her bus.

The address was the same as she'd recorded in Billing. It made her nervous as she got off at her stop in West Greenwich Village. A block up from here, was her meeting. The wind was up and it was sunny after days of rain, so the smell of the city was muted around her. Unlike the subway pong, which she found short of infernal, she liked this smell. Ada meandered a wide street with broad sidewalks and decently sized trees.

It didn't appear to be dangerous here.

But that, she thought, could be a lie.

She walked the street scanning. But... no one hailed her.

Vexing.

She took out her phone to text, on her way back down the street a second time when a small shape on the steps of a reddish brownstone said, "A-Da?"

Ada stopped and peered left.

The kid was 10 or 12-years-old? He had light brown hair, grey eyes with freckles, and a sober expression on his heart-shaped face. And he was in a school uniform sitting there.

"Who are you?"

"Uh. You'd know me from, uh..."

She felt in her pocket for the paperwork she'd taken, "Are you *Fallen-Starscape?*"

"You know... the sunglasses make it hard to see your eyes and..." he shifted a little, "no one around here has piercings."

She took off her glasses with a smile.

He finished, "Everyone around here is stuffy."

"I didn't come up here for everyone else. So, let them judge. I don't care."

He squinted up at her through the sun and decided. "That's cool."

"Oh yeah?" She sized him up. "Well... I expected someone different."

"Not someone who's 11?" He nodded.

"You have to be 13 to play Voice of the Wild." She told him.

"You have to be 13 to play Voice of the Wild in *Co-op mode*," he corrected her. "Like... it's a big distinction. A lot of kids have their own Realms." He gazed down at the tips of his shoes then.

Ada unfolded the paper she'd — yes — taken from Vinnie's desk and scrutinized it. "They might have their own Realms, but they don't have *mammoth* ones, kid. You did."

He didn't look up. And his voice was whispery. "I did."

There was nothing for a moment after that, and Ada glowered at his bowed head. He was upset. She could tell. But she didn't want to crowd him. "The amount of work you must have put into that game Starscape–"

"It's Kent." He rubbed his cheek. "But everyone calls me Kenny."

Ada opened her arms a little, "Do you like that?"

"Uh. No," he said to the step below him.

"All right then, Kent. So, the amount of work you must have put into that place to get it that developed? I measured the footage. That's working on it every day for over 2 years. What... in the hell... happened?" She asked.

His next breath shuddered, and he leaned into the concrete railing a little.

Ada's eyes widened. She turned to sit beside him and open her bag. She had a little bundle of tissues in there since she'd had a lot to cry about lately, and Ada Keller was always ready. But she didn't hand him one. She sat with a few of them in her hands.

She filed it away in her head that it was really hard to sit quietly on a step and listen to an 11-year-old kid cry. It didn't *have* to be your kid. You didn't have to know him. He could be anyone. It just... it sucked. When he cleared up a little, he took the tissues on his own. He wadded them up to his entire face like he wanted to hide.

Ada was not amused, not at all, with whoever had done this. "Tell me what happened, Kent."

"Uh." His voice was a bit thick and unsteady. "Uh... I guess... I started Voice of the Wild like days after it came out. Have... have you been on it that long?"

She didn't turn to him as she replied, "Yes."

"I liked it. I know I was like 9 and all, but I thought I liked how it looked, and I liked the default music and animals and things. And my mom, she used to sit with me while I built stuff. Or, you know, she'd do the books and inventory for the restaurant and I'd build. She'd come over and check everything, you know... she's a *mom*. But she used to tell me I was an artist. An *artist*. So cool. That's back before the Realm was built enough, you know, to *have* a name." He paused and shifted the tissues. "Anyway, I got better at it. Even I could tell. Uh, Voice ran this little online training for their custom build code, and I did that. Then they ran another. I kept doing them. And like, suddenly, I'm in the Advanced Building course with all these like... adults. Do you know what I mean?"

Ada smiled at her own memories. "Oh, *exactly* what you mean."

"My mom, you know, she got busy and moved on from it. She never had a problem with me doing it. But I was putting a lot of time into it. I mean... that's true." He shifted miserably and had to take a breath before he could say, "I was *so proud* of it."

She waited for him to come back from... wherever he went at those words.

"So, I showed it to my dad," he told her. "And I walked him through...

everything I'd done. The drop-in point. The brownstones. The shining city. The bending sea... all of it. A couple of times. I thought he was being quiet because he was impressed. It's so much work to do all that. I can make things in code like... I made something so great."

Now Ada turned her head to peer down at him. He huddled on the steps, more talking to the stone railings than to her. It was the posture of someone defeated.

"And he logged in a night later. Unlocked it. And—"

He couldn't go on. But that was enough for Ada, who had been sitting miles away, licking cheese off her fingers, in the—she now knew—*bubble* of her life. But she had seen the whole thing, the whole stinking crime, the whole dirty betrayal, go down. And so she could forgive herself for sounding a little salty when she said, "Did he even tell you *why*?"

Kent put on a towering, trembling voice, *"You'll never get into law school playing games."*

He tucked his head down, sobbed, and rocked himself. It was a comfort thing. Ada had spent the last few months doing that. The difference was, she was 28. He was *11-years-old,* and his heart had already been broken once. She eyed him. He was *a little kid.*

She flapped out the paper she held. When it blurred in front of her eyes, she wiped her face. Then she started reading, as calmly as she could. He was innately interested in this list. He knew the names of some of the Realms from being on the forums.

Slowly, she got him back.

"Uh—my Japanese sucks. *Watashi no*, uhm-"

"*Watashi no tochuu de*," he rattled off effortlessly. He made a chuckle and rubbed a red-rimmed eye. "It means 'At my place'. I know those guys. It's these 7 guys from this dorm in Japan. They named it because they kept having to rotate whose room they used for building out, and—they said on the forum—they ended up with this huge whiteboard calendar and everyone would sign up and leave a message with 'At my place', and 'At my place'."

"That's cool." Ada realized, and then asked him. "Do you recognize the next one too? You aware of the 8th largest?"

He shook his head shyly. "No."

You sure as hell do.

She handed the paper over to him. "*Breath of the Wild.*" Ada took out her phone and logged in while he beheld the wonder—she bet it was a marvel for him—of inside data on the largest locked Realms in Voice of the Wild.

It sounded horribly sad, yet hauntingly proud. "I was.... *I was number 8*. Me."

"Are. You are." She found the footage she'd sent herself. "You."

He stared up at her, uncomprehending, and Ada handed over her phone. He recognized, and drank in every inch of the display of her recording from earlier in the week. And then he saw the video's *timestamp* and jolted. His eyes were like saucers when he looked up at her.

Ada smiled at him. "Let me tell you what we're gonna do."

IT WAS ONLY A FEW nights later that she stared blankly into her Den. It was fully pink now, with clouds painted everywhere. She'd tried to recreate the kid's flowers and multi-coloured bees with mixed success, but... Ada hoped it would be enough. She hoped *she* would be enough. Finally, she stepped in, walked by the basinet, and checked the air purifier.

If she snuffled the air, it smelled... clean.

She'd been locked in place at the door to this room for too long. Lately, she heard her mom saying *'Ada, you don't have a maternal bone in your body. Everything I passed on to you shriveled up long ago.'* echoing in her head, though somewhere in the last week... it had lost its power.

In the kitchen, her cell phone buzzed. The message said:

How are you doing? Are you at work? Can you look at what I did (BoL)?

(BoL) meant look in *Breath of Life*, which she'd restored under *her* account for Kent. But he had to be *specific* now that he was working on another build (LoF)—*Leap of Faith*. Kent said that he'd named it out of respect for what she'd done. She could pass both builds over to him when he turned 13. He wanted to take them public then.

Ada smiled at the message, went to her kitchen table, and opened her laptop. It always sat there now, cheerfully taking up the space where her boyfriend, Tom, had used to exist. She slid on her virtual reality glasses and raced to the drop-in point Kent had built. She hung in the music and followed the horses. The banner... was now gold. She marveled at how it rippled as it opened. What could she say? The kid was *skilled*.

Breath ~ of ~ Life

By: FallenStarscape
Realm champion: A-Da

The phone buzzed again.

Do you see it, A-Da? What do you think?

It was a bit embarrassing to admit she had to take her hand down from her mouth and wipe her eyes before she could pick up the phone again. She hadn't even been aware a *Realm champion* could be a different user from the creator. Kent was *bright.* She sent a message back.

Yeah, I see it, Kent. It looks good.

It looks great.

I love it.

And she really did.

Despite killing every plant she comes in contact with—even cacti—Karli Stites has envisioned a vibrantly lush garden. Unfortunately, the garden in her story hides terrible secrets.

Will her main character survive this little piece of paradise?

ESCAPE FROM AELLA

Karli Stites

THERE'S THIS MOMENT BETWEEN SLEEPING and waking that's always felt infinite to me. Like if I squeeze my eyes tight enough, if I wish hard enough, if I dream wildly enough, I might be able to escape the hell I'm living. So, each morning when I wake up, I stop time. Every day when the sun comes up, without fail, I lay in bed and let my mind wander. I let myself believe that I didn't grow up unwanted, unloved, and alone. I let myself think that I can do anything. I try to breathe through the pain that constantly surrounds me, wrapping around my heart like a vise, suffocating me until I can barely speak. The time before I open my eyes is the only time I allow myself to let go. Psychologists call it a hypnopompic state, but I call it peace—my sanity.

This morning is like any other. When I wake up, I lay still and breathe slowly, letting myself forget about my problems. I feel limitless; my body isn't my own. I'm no longer Addison Rose Bennett, a girl with no family. In this moment, I'm whoever I want to be. After several minutes of deep breaths, I'm finally ready to face the day.

I open my eyes to darkness.

"What..." I look around with wide eyes. "Where am I?" My voice rings out and fills the silence, but no one answers. It's not surprising since I live alone, but I know I'm not in my bed. My thin mattress is nothing special, but it's softer than the cold surface I'm lying on. I don't know how I got here, but I couldn't have done it alone.

"Wherever here is," I whisper. Again, no one answers. I put my hand on my throat, realizing it's dry and I'm thirsty.

"Hello?" My voice is scratchy and unused like I haven't spoken in a couple days. I know that can't be true because I remember talking to customers at work yesterday.

I'm a mechanic at a local car shop. I work in the back, so I don't get face time with customers too much, but I can't avoid all human interaction, unfortunately. My boss is good about letting me skip out on small talk, though, since he knows I'm awful at it. I recall a particularly pushy customer who flirted obnoxiously with me yesterday, refusing to believe I was a female mechanic who could *actually* fix his car. I roll my eyes. Randy, my boss, had to pull me away before I gave the customer a piece of my mind. Instead of kicking him in the balls like I wanted, I smiled pretty and walked back to the garage.

I cough, trying to clear my throat, but I feel even worse. As a former foster kid, I'm used to getting all the information first: watching my surroundings, observing my peers, and blending into the background. Sometimes it was the difference between being safe and... not. I shiver, shaking off the unpleasant memories.

"No time for that, Addison Rose," I say to myself.

I take another look around, eyes wide, and realize I'm outside. What I suspected might be a dark, dirty basement looks like a... forest? It's still dark, so it's hard to tell, but I can just barely make out tall shapes a short distance away. It looks like I'm sitting in the middle of a clearing—a perfect square—that's surrounded by trees. The overall effect is ominous and makes me feel trapped. I've had my share of bad experiences, but I've never been so confused about what to do next. I bite my lip, debating my options.

For the first time, I look down at the ground to see what I'm sitting on and I startle.

"What the hell..."

Not only is my apartment gone—the same apartment I've rented for myself since I was kicked out of my last group home—but my clothes are gone, too. Luckily, I'm not naked, but I'd probably be more comfortable without clothes on than in the outfit I'm wearing. It's a pure white sundress. Something a pretty, young girl might wear if they went to the beach. Or maybe something I might buy if I had enough money. The unease in my chest builds. *Who would change my clothes?*

Thinking about someone else's hands on my body makes me feel dirty and my skin crawls. The dress is soft and smooth, but I feel uncomfortable, more than I've ever felt in the cheap clothes I usually buy at the thrift store. Not to mention, I'd never pick this dress out for myself; I'm too jaded from my past. I don't deserve to wear something so pure. I'm not meant for something this beautiful. My wardrobe consists of cropped t-shirts, tank tops, jean shorts, tight jeans, leather jackets, and anything else that you'd expect to find on a poor girl who grew up in a bad part of town with no family.

My hair is a blonde so naturally light it almost looks white. I have light grey eyes. I'm covered in tattoos: my left arm has a gorgeous full sleeve in black and grey, and I'm in the middle of finishing my right arm. There's a small stud in my nose and I have a ring pierced through my bottom lip, my left eyebrow, and my belly button. I'm not someone who'd normally wear a pretty, white dress.

But here I am.

"If Randy and the boys could only see me now..." I laugh out loud.

I get so much shit at the shop since I'm the only woman, but I love working there. The guys have only ever seen me covered in grease and oil. When I first started working there, they hit on me all the time, but they learned pretty quickly that I wasn't interested in their advances. Plus, Randy scared them straight when he told them how old I was. I ran away after getting kicked out of my fifth foster home when I was sixteen. Randy saw a poor, homeless kid and took a chance on me, letting me apprentice at his shop until I was old enough to become a fully licensed mechanic. I sigh, wondering if I'll ever see him and the rest of the guys again.

"No need to panic yet, Addi Rose. We've been in worse situations than this and we've been fine," I try to reassure myself, but my voice doesn't sound very encouraging. I want to explore the area more, but I know there's not much I can do in the dark. I'm not interested in falling into a hole and breaking my ankle or getting bitten by a venomous snake. Not that I'm scared of snakes...much.

I decide to lay back down and try to sleep because what else am I going to do? It's too dark to walk around, there's no one for me to talk to, and I know if I stay awake, I'm only going to panic and spiral. And hey, maybe when I wake up, I'll be back in my tiny bed. Maybe the next time I open my eyes, I'll see the plain, peeling white walls of my shitty apartment. Maybe, this will all be a dream. I'll go to work tomorrow, tell the guys, and we'll laugh about how funny I'd look in a pretty, white dress. Yeah, maybe...

THE NEXT TIME I WAKE up, it's light outside. The memories of last night start rushing back. I don't open my eyes. Not yet. I want to pretend for a little longer. *If I don't open my eyes, then nothing's wrong, right?* I can imagine that I'm still in bed at home. It's like any other day. I'm doing my usual morning routine. I'm stopping time. Breathe in. Breathe out. Nothing is wrong. Nothing is wrong. Nothing. Is. Wrong.

But I can only lie to myself for so long. I can't fake it forever. There's going to be a time when I'll have to pull myself together and face the day.

That time is now.

I'm ready.

When I open my eyes, I exhale slowly. I sit up and look around, stiffening when I see the clearing in the daylight. It's beautiful but still unsettling. I'm lying on a soft bed of moss in the exact center of the meadow. It's a perfect square. A *perfect* square—obviously man-made, no doubt about it. Large trees surround me, each of them planted an equal distance apart from each other and the center of the square. It's eerie and unnatural. The trees are close together, but I could easily squeeze through them.

I wonder what's on the other side...

I squint, startling when I notice some colorful fruit hanging off the trees. I scan my eyes around the rest of the square. My eyes widen. They're *all* fruit trees.

"Hmm, interesting." I'm not sure why someone would put me in the middle of a square full of fruit trees, but I'm not exactly complaining. Not yet at least. It could be worse.

I decide to do a full scan of the area before I start exploring. I find bushes and smaller shrubs which seem to have growths on them. I wonder if those have some sort of food source on them, too. Maybe nuts? I put them on my list of things to check out. My eyes continue scanning the area.

"Jackpot!" I yell. At the far end of the clearing, I see a giant, glittering pool of water and a small trickling waterfall. I race over to it. My second spell of sleep has only increased my thirst. The square isn't too big, so it only takes me a few minutes to reach the pool. I run straight to the small waterfall, intending to open my mouth right under the stream, but stop before I ingest anything.

Wait, what the hell am I doing? I'm in an unknown place. And this is an unknown body of water. Am I really going to drink this water?

I look at the water warily. It looks clean, clear, and delicious. I put my hand under the stream and let it run down my skin. It feels cool and refreshing. My skin doesn't burn or anything, so it's obviously not poison.

Well, that's a relief.

"Maybe, I can try a tiny drop?" I don't know who I'm asking since I'm the only one here, but it feels better to speak out loud sometimes.

I nod, answering my own question. I cup my hands under the stream and catch some water, taking a tiny sip. It's amazing. I'm so thirsty and I need more, but I hold back.

I wait five minutes. Nothing happens. I want to make sure I'm not going to drop dead from drinking random forest water, so I wait another ten minutes. At this point, my throat is burning, and I decide that I'm so thirsty I don't care anyway, so I fill up my cupped hands and take another drink. I spend five full minutes filling and emptying my hands until I'm satisfied.

"Let's hope that wasn't a mistake," I say.

My stomach grumbles. I look down and pat my belly, sighing.

I wish I could hold off a little longer to eat because I still don't feel comfortable ingesting anything my kidnapper provided for me, but now that I've had water, I realize I'm starving.

When's the last time I ate? I feel like the only thing I've done since I woke up to darkness is ask questions. Where? When? Why?

I usually try not to dwell too much on the past. I leave that to the moments between sleeping and waking—that Addison Rose has the luxury of thinking about the past and the future. But I can't do that in my everyday life. I'm a young woman living on her own, trying to survive. If I let myself sink into the past, I'll drown. If I let myself dream too much, I'll be disappointed. So, I live in the moment.

It's all I have.

Having all this time to myself is making me anxious. I don't want to *think*. I want to *do something*. I like action. I like adrenaline. I'm not one to sit around. That's why I started getting tattoos, piercings, and dressing in edgy clothes when I was only fifteen. Growing up, I was targeted for my looks. I was... too pretty. Too innocent looking. My lip curls at the vile men that my young self was subjected to. Despite the odds, I survived. I made it out. And as soon as I could, I found a way to protect myself against predators. Today, I wear my body art like armor. It makes me feel safe.

I sigh. This damn place isn't good for me. I can't stop *thinking*.

"I don't want to be here," I whisper. I feel more vulnerable than I've felt in years, and I hate it. I decide to push everything back like I always do and act. I stand up, deciding to walk the perimeter and take inventory of all the fruit trees and shrubs. I'm hungry and I figure if someone put in the effort to put me here, they probably don't want to kill me off with expired food. Right? It makes sense in my head, anyway.

I turn away from the waterfall and walk to the closest tree. I raise my eyebrows. There's a huge variety of fruit, but it's like nothing I've seen before. Once again, I'm wondering where the hell I am. Someone has obviously gone to great lengths to keep me hidden and they must have traveled far, because I think I'm in an entirely new ecosystem. Somewhere tropical, maybe?

When I reach the tree next to the pool, I pluck a piece of fruit right off a low-hanging branch. I purse my lips, cocking my head in confusion.

"This is so annoying," I mutter. "I'm starting to get a complex."

I may only be eighteen, but I think my childhood has helped me grow wise beyond my years. I like to think I'm clever, but I'm honestly stumped. Not only do I have absolutely *no idea* where I am, I have *no freaking clue* what the hell I'm staring at. It looks like an apple, I guess, if an apple was bright blue and covered in raised pink polka dots. So, nothing like an apple.

Maybe I'm in South America? Do they have fruit like this? I'm not sure because I dropped out of high school when I was sixteen. Although, I don't think they teach this kind of thing in school. I'm still a little unsure, but it looks relatively harmless. And the water was fine. I'm not dead, at least. It's probably some sort of sweet fruit. It smells sweet, so I imagine it'll taste the same.

Shrugging, I take a bite. And promptly spit it out. It's disgusting. It tastes nothing like I expected. It's waxy and hard. Unfortunately, not hard enough that it stopped me from sinking my teeth into it. I cough a little, trying to get the taste out of my mouth, but it lingers. I drop the colorful fruit to the ground and back away, glaring at it like it personally offended me.

"Bastard fruit." I pull up the bottom of my dress and wipe my hands on my bare legs. It's not very ladylike, but I never claimed to be a lady. When I drop my dress and rub my hands together, I raise an eyebrow because my hands feel extra soft.

I have a hunch, so I reach my right hand up to my face and sniff it.

"Oh, yes." I bend over and grab the *fruit.*

"Because you're not actually fruit, are you? You're soap." I hum in satisfaction. Nodding my head, I walk back over to the water and kneel over the little pool. I submerge my hands in the water and scrub. When suds start forming, I know I'm right.

"Ha!" I jump up and do a little dance. The sound of my yell bounces off the nearby trees, and I stop. For a second, I forgot where I was. Even though I uncovered one mystery, I'm still nowhere near answering the rest of my questions. The most pressing one being *where the hell am I?* I'm still lost. Kidnapped. Whatever you want to call it.

At least this soap will come in handy if I end up being stuck here for a while. I'm planning on escaping the first chance I get, but it never hurts to be prepared. If my kidnapper is going to provide me with somewhere to wash up, I'm not going to refuse. I don't know why they'd give me soap, but I can't say I've been treated poorly so far. This setup is better than any of the foster homes I lived in growing up. Not like those are very hard to beat.

I turn away from the water so I can check out more trees. I decide to christen my new home the "Garden" because I'm sick of calling it *the square, the clearing,* or whatever else weird-ass names I've been saying in my head. Since all I've seen around me besides my bathing pool are fruit trees and shrubs, the name seems appropriate. Besides, no one else is around to tell me any different.

The next set of trees I come across has another type of "fruit" on them. They look like bananas, but they're neon green. I'm wary since the last thing I tried wasn't *actually* edible, but I can't think of another option to figure out what it is. This time, though, I only take a small bite—the tiniest bite I can. I let out a breath of relief when I don't want to spit it out. Surprisingly, the green banana tastes like nuts. Not just one type of nut, though; it tastes like a mix of every nut I've ever eaten. Kind of weird, but I'll take it.

I take the nut banana with me and munch on it while I continue walking. When I come to a corner, the nut banana trees stop, and I see a new type of tree.

"Hmm, interesting."

I look back and notice a pattern that I missed before. The Garden is a perfect square with the bathing pool and waterfall in one corner. There's one tree on either side of the pool with soap fruit. The nut banana trees are lined up on one full side of the Garden. I suspect that the other three sides each have their own type of tree. I also see bushes and shrubs tucked into each of the remaining three corners, which I suspect have some sort of food or useful substance for me to use. The middle of the Garden is pretty much empty, except for the moss bed I woke up on and some flowers.

Someone obviously took great care in setting this up. It's gorgeous, practical, and efficient. It scares me because the more I think about it, the more I realize I could exist here for years all alone. No one ever needs to come in and give me more food or clothes. I have everything I need. It's a self-sustaining environment. I can be here alone forever, and no one will ever know except my captor. No one will ever find me.

"Say goodbye to any escape plans you've been forming in the back of your mind, Addi Rose," I whisper.

I kind of want to drop to the floor and cry, but I'm not a crier and I'm *definitely not* a quitter. So, I ignore my moment of weakness and continue walking.

LATER THAT DAY, I'VE DISCOVERED "vegberry" trees—trees with small vegetables that look exactly like fuzzy orange blueberries—and meat trees, which are even weirder than you'd think. The meat fruit looks extremely unusual, even though it kind of tastes like chicken. I was skeptical before I tried the crimson red triangle, and my mouth literally dropped open in surprise when I realized it was some sort of meat. How's that possible?

No idea. I've decided to accept the Garden is peculiar and there are things I can't explain.

The remaining side of the Garden is lined with trees that have fruit that *actually* tastes like fruit. Funnily enough, the real fruit looks the least like real fruit. It's shaped like a mango, but it's brown, rough, and scaly. Honestly, it kind of feels like a snake, but it's delicious. I call it snake fruit.

Now that I've finished taking inventory of my fruit trees, I'm bored. I pick up a snake fruit, take a big bite, and walk back towards the vegberry trees. I decide to get some more, because why not? I also want to peek through the trees and see if I can see anything. When I was looking for food and supplies, I didn't go exploring beyond a preliminary search, but I'm ready to take a deeper look. Maybe I can find a way out?

"Yeah, probably not," I huff.

It doesn't take me too long to walk to the other side. I'm standing in front of the vegberry trees in no time, plucking a few pieces off and popping them in my mouth one at a time.

"Now, let's see what we can find back here," I say.

I slip through the trees. It's instantly darker. I expected it, but the difference between the Garden and this hidden world is profound. Still, I feel safer back here. Like the trees are watching my back. It's probably a stupid sentiment because I'm sure there are cameras everywhere and my kidnapper is watching my every move, but I feel better in the trees. The darkness is my friend. I've never felt that way before. It's always been my enemy, but I like feeling the blackness wrap around me like a blanket. I smile, and it feels like coming home.

Surprisingly, the forest goes a little further back than I expected.

I walk for another minute before I come to a barrier. And it's a *freaking barrier.* A glass wall. There's a *glass wall in the middle of the forest.* When I first realized I was in a garden paradise, I thought there'd be a fence. Not a damn glass wall.

"What the hell..."

I look up. I can't tell how far up it goes, because it's *glass*, but I have a sinking feeling that it's *really freaking high.* My gut churns. Am I...in a *box?* I laugh nervously.

No...that can't be right. There's no way. *There's just. No. Way.*

My hands start to sweat. I wipe them on my dress.

I groan.

"My god, the dress. I forgot about this stupid dress."

I suddenly start to panic, my breath coming fast, imagining some sick bastard taking off my clothes, putting me in a white dress, and shoving me in a glass box. I know I'm hyperventilating at this point, but I can't stop.

"Wow! I'm sure you're having a laugh right now, you psycho!" I scream.

My skin starts to itch, and I want to strip out of my dress, but I don't have anything else to wear. Even though this guy has already seen me naked, I'm not letting him see me like that again. I gag thinking about him getting a sneak peek when I was passed out.

"I bet you're watching, huh?"

"Disgusting," I mutter. "You're a piece of shit! You know that, right?" I'm screaming pretty loudly at this point, stomping around the forest and having a full-on tantrum. It's impressive.

"What do you want from me? I don't have anything! I'm not worth anything. So, if you want a ransom or something, you're not going to get anything."

I pause. "Maybe I shouldn't have said that." I roll my eyes at myself, but I keep going.

"If you want me to touch you or something, think again, asshole! Greater men than you have tried, and they've ended up on the floor holding their balls." I narrow my eyes and cross my arms. "You may have gotten a free pass when you put me in this dress, but try again, and I'll mess you up. You won't be getting shit from me, dude. I'd rather *die* than touch you. I've survived worse than you, buddy. You took the wrong girl, and you'll be sorry."

"I believe that."

I whip around, turning my head towards the deep voice behind me. "Hello?"

I hear a rustling sound and a huge figure comes walking out of the trees in front of me. My mouth drops open, and my eyebrows disappear into my hairline. There's someone else here. I'm not alone. I almost run forward, but then I remember that there's a glass wall in front of me and I have no idea who this guy is. For all I know, he's the one who kidnapped me.

Before I get too excited, I give him a wary look. "Who are you?"

"I'm X," he answers.

"X?" I ask, pursing my lips. His lips quirk for a second like he knows I think his name is a little weird, but he doesn't comment. "I'm Addison Rose."

He nods. "Pretty."

I roll my eyes. He smiles a little.

"Not much of a talker, are you?" He shrugs again. Okay, then.

"So, what are you doing here? How did you get here? Why are we in these glass boxes? Do you know who took us? Where are we?" I shoot off the questions in rapid-fire.

X's eyes are wide open by the end of my interrogation. He starts to shrug but stops himself when he sees my face.

He smiles a little, looking sheepish. "Sorry, I'm not used to talking. I haven't spoken to someone else in...years?"

My mouth drops open in shock. "Years?"

"Well, besides the Others, but they don't count..." His voice trails off and he looks sad. Broken. Utterly destroyed. My heart aches for him, and I know without a doubt that he's innocent. He's a victim, just like me. Hell, even more than me. He needs my help. I feel an instant kinship with him. Maybe it's all the years I spent in foster care that left me feeling sad and broken, too, but I think I can relate to X in a way that I've never been able to relate to anyone else before.

My voice is a little soft when I respond. I raise my hand up to the glass barrier.

"It's okay, X. You can talk to me now." I smile. And his returning smile is beautiful. It might even be the most beautiful thing I've ever seen in my shitty life. When he raises his hand, lining it up to mine on his side of the glass wall, it feels right. It feels like coming home.

"SO, HOW LONG HAVE YOU been here?" I ask.

X and I are lying against the glass wall facing each other. Up this close, it's easier to make out what he looks like, even in the dark. He's huge.

I'm slightly above average height for a woman, but he looks like he's seven feet tall. He's built like a bodybuilder: extremely muscular and well defined. I don't know what the hell he's been doing in captivity, but it's working. He's also shirtless. I don't know if our kidnappers—the Others—decided not to give him a shirt or if he prefers not to wear one, but I don't ask.

His upper body is covered in tattoos. I wonder where he got them. Do they mean something? They look kind of tribal to me, but it's hard to tell in the dark. He has short black hair, cropped close to his head on the sides, with a little extra length on top. His eyes almost seem to glow a little bit, which is weird, but mostly cool. They're an unusual color—like warm, melted caramel. He has scars on his face, which I wonder about, but again, I don't ask. There's one cutting through his right eyebrow, one on the bridge of his nose, and one running from the corner of his left eye to the middle of his cheek.

X takes a while to respond, which I expect. I can tell that he's thinking about his answer. He's not used to talking, and he doesn't seem like the kind of person to waste words.

"All my life. Or what I can remember of it, at least. I've never known anything different than this," he answers. The sadness in his voice breaks my heart. *All his life.*

"I'm sorry, X," I say, because I don't know what else to say.

He looks confused at my response. "Why? It's not your fault."

I sigh. "Yeah. It's just something we say when we don't know what to say. It just means that I'm sorry that happened to you. I'm sorry this is happening to you. I feel for you. I'm here for you."

"Oh." He hums. "I'm sorry, Addison Rose."

I laugh. "For what, X?"

He looks at me seriously. "For the same. You were taken from your home, too."

I smile. "That's true. But it was never really home, I guess." I sigh and lean back into the grass, stretching my arms above my head. I turn my head back to X and find him watching me. "Thanks, X." He smiles.

"Can you tell me more about the Others?" I ask after a few minutes of silence. X takes a deep breath.

"Yes, Addison Rose, I can, but you won't like it."

I shiver. His tone is ominous, and I know what he's about to tell me will change my life forever.

"Yes." I nod. "I need to know. Please tell me."

"The Others run Aella," he starts slowly.

"Aella?" I interrupt.

"This place." He pauses. "Aella is a hub for all things...unnatural. If people pay for it, they'll do it. Aella caters to the most depraved, disgusting, sadistic beings. The Others have a hand in all illegal trades: slavery, sex trading, breeding, fighting, and more. Aella is their one-stop-shop."

He grimaces. "They call this place the Zoo. They have hundreds, maybe even thousands, of captives—*exhibits*—kept in these glass enclosures ready and ripe for the picking. People come, and they can watch us, they can buy us—they can do whatever they want with us."

I'm horrified at the end of X's speech.

This can't be real. No, no, no, no, no.

I'm starting to panic again, but I don't want X to think I'm weak, so I try not to let it show.

But X sees right through me. "Are you okay?"

I'm hyperventilating, and I feel like I'm going to pass out. I'm definitely *not okay,* but I give him a thumbs up anyway.

X looks worried. He scoots forward, pressing his body up to the glass, but he still can't touch me because we're separated by a wall. I wish we *could* touch because I desperately need something—someone—to ground me right now. But he can't. No one can.

Never again.

Because I'll be stuck in this glass box forever. My breath comes faster, and I start to see black spots.

"Addison Rose!" X shouts at me, but his voice isn't breaking the thick haze that's descended over me. "Addison Rose, listen to me. I heard you earlier. You're strong. You can do this. You'll be fine. Just breathe. Breathe. We got this. You and me. We'll be fine. Just breathe, okay?"

X keeps talking. After a couple of minutes, I start to calm down. My vision clears, and I start breathing normally. I look into X's eyes and they're blazing brightly, the glow practically inhuman. It's gorgeous.

I settle down a little more, smiling sheepishly. "I'm sorry, I don't know what came over me. That was weird."

"There's nothing to be ashamed of. I've had years to come to terms with my situation. You've been here less than a day. I think you're doing fine," he says.

"You're right." I nod.

I feel a little better, although I'm still kind of embarrassed. I've never done anything like that before, especially in front of someone else. I keep everything locked up tight. And I never let anyone in. That's my thing. X is breaking down my barriers, and I'm not entirely sure if I should be worried or not.

I decide to ignore all the feelings talk and get back to business.

"So, you said the Others have their hand in all these illegal trades, right? Does that mean that we're targeted for something specific?"

X looks uncomfortable for the first time since we met. Suddenly, I'm wary. If he's uncomfortable, it's probably not a good sign.

I swallow. "X, come on. What is it? Do you know what they're going to do to me?"

He sighs. "No. I don't, but I can guess. Based on your gender, you'll probably be used as a breeder."

"So, they'd impregnate me? Make me have babies?"

"Normally, yes, that *would* be the case. But I don't think they'll do that with you. They'll probably take some of your eggs and implant them in other breeders and maybe some of your DNA for splicing, but I'd guess based on your... looks—" he blushes, "they'll want you for the sex trade."

Well, shit.

THE NEXT MORNING, I'M STILL freaking out about my potential future as a sex slave. X and I spent the rest of the night exchanging stories about our childhood. Mine was full of depressing tales about a poor, unloved, pretty, young girl who was always running away from men who wanted to violate her. And X's was full of loneliness, blood, and pain.

Ah, what a pair we make.

X doesn't know his heritage. He has no clue where he's from. No idea what his real name is. In the dark last night, he confessed that the Others always referred to him as "Exhibit D-988657475203-01" growing up, so he thought that was his name. When he got a little older, he realized he was wrong; he'd never had a name. So, he gave himself one. I don't know how it's possible for a story to break my heart and put it back together at the same time, but I think that one does.

"So, when is something going to happen?"

X quirks an eyebrow. "What do you mean?"

"Well, this is my second day, but I haven't done anything except eat, sleep, and talk to you. Are the Others going to come by at any moment and force me to have sex with someone?"

"No," X answers. "It's not going to happen all the time. Like I said, there are a lot of people here. Lots of *exhibits*. So, some people might only get called once a week. It depends on popularity, I guess." He looks at me and grimaces. "You'll probably be pretty popular, though. Especially at the beginning."

"Why!" I exclaim.

"Well, new exhibits are always popular." I nod. "But you'll be extra popular because you're beautiful. And unique. You're special. They've never had anyone like you here before."

X says it like it's a fact, not like he's trying to compliment me. I try to hold his gaze, but I chicken out and look away. I'm *not* good at feelings. I clear my throat. When I look back, he's smiling a little. I pretend to cough.

"What happens when I'm *called*?"

His smile drops and he looks serious again. "You'll be brought to the Transfer Room."

"What?"

"The Transfer Room. It's a long rectangular room right behind the meat trees," he explains. "On the other side of that is the viewing room. For you, it will be a *Playroom.*"

I hear the disgust in his tone, and I feel my skin crawl because I can only imagine what type of playing takes place in that room.

"You'll go in the Transfer Room and get ready in there. Everything you need will be there based on what the guest paid for. Sometimes you may even stay there if the guest didn't pay enough to get the full experience. Then, they'll just watch. If you end up going into the viewing room, you'll have specific guidelines and rules to follow. The Others don't want you to give up more than the bare minimum. If the guest wants more, they'll need to shell out more money."

I want to throw up. X looks sympathetic, but there's nothing he can do. There's nothing anyone can do. We're both stuck here.

"What if I refuse?"

He gives me a look.

"Torture and death. Got it," I mutter.

I know I said before that I'd rather die than touch the sick bastard who kidnapped me, but that was before. Before I met X. Sure, we're on separate sides of a glass wall and we're never going to touch and we're both messed up and broken, but I don't want to just *die.* Not anymore.

Do I have to do this? Am I *really* going to do this?

I look at X, desperately scrambling for a new topic. I don't want to think about what I'll have to do when they call me. "What do you do for the Others?"

"I fight."

I roll my eyes and huff out a laugh. "Can you elaborate?"

He smiles a little. "I'm a gladiator. I fight. My viewing room is an Arena. Guests pay to watch my matches and bet. For my exhibition matches, guests bring people they want me to fight—prisoners or other strong warriors—or they just choose people that are already here in other exhibits. Sometimes they even bring wild animals. There are no rules."

My mouth drops open. "Wow, that's insane." I look him over. "I can't say I'm surprised. It sounds dangerous though."

He nods. "It is. All the matches are no surrender."

I gulp. "You mean…"

"Fight to the death."

"Shit."

Suddenly, I'm stupidly scared for young X. I wish I could go back in time and wrap him up in a blanket. I want to hold his hand and tell him it's going to be okay. I inch a little closer to the glass and put my hand up, laying it flat like I did last night. X copies my movement. "I'm sorry, X."

He smiles a little. "I'm sorry, Addison Rose."

We're silent for a few more minutes. I'm about to speak again, but I stop when I hear a terrible sound.

"Exhibit E-988657475203-01, make your way to the Transfer Room immediately."

At first, I don't realize it's me. That awful, computerized voice can't be talking about me. But then I realize that X can't hear it. I cock my head as the voice repeats again and again.

"Do you hear that?" X looks confused for a second, but his face clears with realization and then dread. He shakes his head sadly.

"No," he says. Or he tries to, but I can't hear over the screaming in my ear.

"I can't hear you!" I yell.

"Exhibit E-988657475203-01, make your way to the Transfer Room immediately."

I put my hands over my ears to try and block out the noise, but it doesn't work. Where the hell is it coming from?

I look at X, scared out of my mind that I'll never see him again. He looks at me the same way. I don't know what to do.

"Exhibit E-988657475203-01, make your way to the Transfer Room immediately."

Shit. I know what I need to do.

I walk away.

I turn back and see X has his hand on the glass. I stop.

"Exhibit E-988657475203-01, make your way to the Transfer Room immediately."

I leave.

I WALK INTO THE TRANSFER Room with my head held high. As soon as I touched the glass wall, the barrier disappeared, and I fell inside. The room is long and skinny: the same length as the Garden, but only about ten feet wide. At one end, I see a bathroom and I rush over. Inside, there's a toilet, sink, and a full shower. The shower looks freaking amazing, and I'm gross after hanging out in the forest for almost two days, so I'm tempted to use it.

Maybe I can take a shower and pretend I'm alone? I'm good at pretending. I see a fresh pile of clothes on the counter, and I make my decision. Yes, please to being clean. I don't want to make it too easy for these freaks, though, so I take a super speedy shower, washing my hair and body with a single-minded ferocity.

I reach my arm out, looking for a towel, but I don't find anything fluffy and soft. Poking my head out, I scan the room.

"You've got to be shitting me."

These bastards tricked me. There aren't any towels. Classy.

I grab the clean clothes off the counter and pull them over my head. Not surprisingly, it's another dress. This one is light grey, almost the same shade as my eyes. It's also much more indecent than the last dress. With my long hair dripping wet down me, it looks practically obscene.

"Well played," I say, raising my middle finger in the air. I don't know where the cameras are, but I'm sure they're somewhere in this room.

I brush my teeth, noticing the toothpaste comes out of something that looks like a pink grape.

After I'm clean, I leave the bathroom. I ignore the Playroom, pretending it doesn't exist. Like I said, I'm good at pretending. I figure a guest is just paying to watch me this time since I haven't been called into the Playroom. Unless I'm still supposed to be *getting ready*?

There's a long couch in here, a few small chairs, and a table. There's also a bed. The bed doesn't have any sheets on it, but they're sitting in a folded pile on the mattress. Am I supposed to make the bed or something?

I decide to make the bed. It takes me a little longer than it usually does at my apartment because this bed is much bigger than my twin and the sheets are kind of unusual, but I finish in ten minutes. Then I'm left with nothing else to do.

I look around the room, but nothing else speaks to me. I don't see any other outstanding tasks. I put my hand on the bed and press down. It feels comfortable.

"What the hell," I mutter. I take a running jump and catapult myself up onto the bed. It's *really* comfortable. The softest, nicest bed I've ever laid in. I smile. Job well done, Addi Rose. I burrow under the covers and fall asleep.

I OPEN MY EYES TO darkness. My chest pounds hard, and I sit up.

"Where am I?" I call out into the silence. "What's going on? Hello?"

All my memories come rushing back and I remember. Aella. The Others. The Zoo.

X.

"I need to find him."

I stand up, wobbling on unsteady legs for a second before I right myself. How did I even get back here? The last thing I remember is going to sleep in the Transfer Room. And then nothing. I have no idea how long it's been. I don't know what happened after I went to sleep. I don't know anything. All I know is I need to see X.

I make it to the vegberry trees in a few minutes and then I'm walking up to the glass barrier a minute later. As I get closer, I see X pacing in front of the wall. I want to stop and admire him, but I don't want him worrying about me for another second. I'd be out of my mind if he was the one called away.

He stops moving as soon as he sees me, running up as close as he can to the glass wall.

"Addison Rose!" He puts his hand up and I follow suit. "I've been so worried." He runs his eyes all over my face and then my body, checking to make sure I'm okay. He pauses when he realizes I'm in different clothes. "Did they do anything to you?"

"No, I'm fine, X. It's okay. No one touched me, I swear."

He looks skeptical, but nods.

"What happened?" He asks.

"It was just a viewing thing, I guess. They just wanted to...watch me." I shrug. My cheeks heat a little bit. "They had new clothes out for me in the bathroom. They wanted to watch me shower and clean myself. And then they had me make the bed. And then I just slept. It was weird. No one asked me to do anything else. No one even spoke to me. I woke up later in the Garden and came straight to you."

X looks worried, but also relieved. "Hmm, well, that's not bad. Better than we hoped for."

I nod enthusiastically. "Absolutely."

We both go quiet, and I drop to the ground. He takes a seat next to me. "It's kind of messed up, though, right?"

X looks over at me. "What is?"

"The fact that I'm happy some creep just watched me shower and sleep. Because it's better than the alternative."

He sighs. "I'm sorry, Addison Rose."

I look at him, thinking about his experience in the gladiator area, forced to fight and kill.

"I'm sorry, X."

THE NEXT TIME THEY CALL for me, I'm not ready. I don't think one is ever really ready to be called back to a room called the Playroom to be a sex slave, though. It's just so easy to get lost talking to X that I forgot what I was here for.

I know as soon as I step into the Transfer Room that this time will be different. The outfit laid out for me in the bathroom is ridiculous. I put it on and stare in the mirror, scoffing at my reflection. It's all barely there and black straps. The result is that I look basically naked, with a side of *I'd never wear this in a million years.*

When I leave the bathroom, the door to the Playroom is open. I gulp. Shit. I don't want to do this. The last time I was here, I didn't look. I purposely didn't look. I didn't want to see some psycho staring at me. But now, I have to go out there and pretend to be a docile little sex slave. Or this dude is going to freaking torture and murder me. That would suck. X would be all alone again. I can't leave him all alone. He needs me.

I take a deep breath and give myself a pep talk. "You got this, Addi Rose."

That's it. That's the pep talk. I said I wasn't big on feelings, and I meant it.

I walk slowly into the Playroom. It's dark, but not like it is in the forest. I think this lighting is called *mood lighting*. Gross. It's amber, muted to cast a mysterious glow. There's a giant bed—California King at least—in here that puts the one in the Transfer Room to shame. Even from here, I can tell the sheets are silky and smooth. They're blood-red. Creepy, much?

There's a long table with a random assortment of food and a small table next to it, but I ignore both of those. I'm not hungry. I also ignore the wall that's full of...toys. I really don't want to know what most of those do. My eyes continue to roam the room until I finally find the other occupant of the room, and they almost bug out when I see what he looks like.

What. The. Hell.

This dude is orange. Orange. Not orange like he went a little overboard on his last spray tan, but orange like a damn Cheeto. Bright freaking orange. My mouth drops open.

"Uhm," I start. Am I supposed to say something?

"Hello." His voice is rumbly and deep. Very unusual. It sounds unnatural.

"I'm Addison Rose," I say because I don't know what else to do, and I feel awkward. He cocks his head.

"Addissson Rossse," he repeats. It sounds weird, but I chalk it up to an accent.

"So, are you an actor or something?"

He cocks his head again.

"An actor," I saw slowly. "Like in movies or on television?"

"No," he finally answers. Okay, then.

I'm still not sure what I'm supposed to do. I look around the room helplessly. I walk over to the food table. I'm thirsty, so I figure I'll at least get something to drink while I'm stuck hanging out with Cheeto guy. I pick up a glass of water from the table and take a sip. Out of the corner of my eye, I see a piece of something that looks a little like chocolate. I lick my lips. Yum.

Suddenly, before I can blink, I'm on the bed, flat on my back. Orange guy is hovering over me, his nose in my neck. He's sniffing me. Sniffing! Me! He licks my neck. Licks. My. Neck. There's a rip in the middle of his tongue, and I'm so scared I feel like I'm going to pee myself.

When he comes back up for air, his pupils are narrowed into slits like a mother freaking snake. He has snake eyes. Holy shit.

Not going to lie, I push him off and run screaming from the room like a little bitch.

I scream, and I scream, and I scream all the way through the vegberry trees and to the glass wall. X is waiting for me when I get there. I come to a stop, leaning over my knees, panting for breath.

X's eyes widen dramatically when he sees me in my Girls Gone Wild outfit and he blushes a little, but he quickly gets down to business when he realizes how freaked out I am.

"What happened?"

"Guy...orange...snake...lick...sniff..."

X is understandably confused by my attempt at an explanation. I take a few deep breaths. *Okay, so I guess I need to work out more.* I take a few more deep breaths. When I have my breathing under control, I start again.

"There was this guy. He was bright orange. Like really, really orange. And he was weird, which I expected, but he seemed kind of shy at first, which was good since I didn't want to *do* anything, right? But then, he just randomly freaked out and rushed me over to the bed. Super fast. He jumped on top of me and started sniffing me and licking me. His tongue was forked, and he had eyes like a freaking snake! I was so scared, X. I ran out of there. He didn't chase me or anything, but I'm worried I'm going to get in trouble."

When I finish my story, I expect X to do his thing where he tells me everything will be okay, blah, blah, blah. But he doesn't. Instead, he looks worried.

"Why do you look like that, X? This guy was just a weirdo, right? Just some method actor who dyes his skin orange and gets weird contacts and forks his tongue. And then he preys on poor, innocent girls like me."

X furrows his eyebrows. "No, Addison Rose. That guy was Serpenten." He pauses. "I'm surprised one of them is here. They don't visit Aella too often because their galaxy is kind of far away. There's probably a whole bunch of them here. I doubt he came all this way alone. Although, I heard you're the first person abducted from your planet. A big-ticket item, I guess. He might have come alone if he wanted to snag you for himself…"

My tiny mind explodes into a rainbow of color. All of X's words run a marathon in my head. Serpenten. Galaxy. Abducted. Planet.

What.

The.

Hell.

"Excuse me, X?" I smile sweetly.

He smiles back. He doesn't realize yet that this smile is not a happy smile.

"Did you say Serpenten? Galaxy?"

X looks confused again. "Yes?"

"What exactly did you mean by that?"

He gulps. "Uh, what?"

"Are you telling me that Aella is not, in fact, a place, but that it's actually a freaking planet?"

"No..." he starts. I raise an eyebrow. He smiles sheepishly. "It's a moon."

"Oh. My. God." I kind of want to scream. So, I do. "You've got to be kidding me. You never thought to tell me that Aella wasn't on Earth?!"

"Earth?" He asks.

"Oh my god." I slap a hand to my face. "Please tell me you know what Earth is."

He shrugs.

"Wow." I pace around the area, muttering to myself and throwing my hands up. No wonder I don't recognize any of these stupid fruits. I can't believe I thought I was in South America. I'm so stupid. I spend the next ten minutes ranting and muttering to myself under my breath about aliens, moons, and evil orange assholes.

"So, when you say you don't know your heritage... you mean that you don't know what planet you're from?"

X shakes his head sadly. I kind of want to cry. He doesn't even know what species he is. That's awful.

"Well, you look human to me. That's what I am. We look similar. Although, you look extra big and muscle-y," I note. He laughs. "Who cares what you are anyway? Not me. We're sticking together."

I put my hand on the glass. He does the same. We smile at each other.

"Exhibit E-988657475203-01, make your way to the Transfer Room immediately. Prepare for transport."

My eyes open wide. "Oh my god. X!" I feel tears burning in my eyes for the first time in years. I don't want to leave. I can't leave.

"X, they're sending me away. I'm being sold!"

X's eyes burn brighter than I've ever seen. His skin ripples and vibrates with energy.

"Exhibit E-988657475203-01, make your way to the Transfer Room immediately. Prepare for transport."

"X, what do I do?" My eyes continue to burn, but I don't dare let them fall. I can't be weak. Not when this is the last time I'll see him. Only after I'm gone. Only then will I let myself cry. He points towards the Transfer Room, and we walk together, keeping tight to the glass.

I try not to panic, but it's hard because I just *know* that the Serpenten guy is waiting for me on the other side of the door.

We keep walking.

"Exhibit E-988657475203-01, make your way to the Transfer Room immediately. Prepare for transport."

When we reach the Transport Room, I turn to X one last time. I stare into his caramel eyes. I wish we could touch. I want to press my hand against his with no glass between us. Give him a hug and tell him that everything is going to be okay.

Through the glass door, I see the distinct orange skin of my new owner. He can't see me yet, but I know he's looking. He's waiting for me to come out. X's eyes are tormented. He puts his other hand up and I mirror him.

For the first time in my life, I stop time while I'm awake. It's not the moment between sleeping and waking that feels infinite. It's right now. It's this time with X. I dream of a world where he doesn't have to fight to the death, where I'm not sold off to the highest bidder, where we're not kept apart in glass cages. I dream we have a future.

And for the first time in ten years, I cry.

When I turn away, I shut off my emotions. This is the last time I'll let myself feel. This is the last time I'll allow *anything* to break through my walls. Never again.

Just before the last brick slides into place, locking away my heart forever, I hear a roar. It's a bestial roar that's so loud, I imagine the entirety of Aella can hear it. My heart beats faster because I recognize the roar. I turn around just in time to see a *dragon* burst out of X's skin. X's gorgeous, hulking, tattooed, tanned body is gone and in its place is a huge black dragon with caramel eyes.

"Holy shit," I breathe.

And just when I think it can't get any crazier, he breathes *freaking fire* and the glass wall burns. Before I can get hurt, the black dragon flies towards me and snatches me up in a giant clawed hand. Normally, I might be a little concerned, but I know this dragon is X, and X would *never* hurt me. So, I settle in for a nice long ride in a dragon's claw.

I did *not* see that coming.

A FEW HOURS LATER, X lands on a mountain. I started panicking when we first left the Zoo because I thought I was going to suffocate in the moon's atmosphere, but I should've trusted X. He obviously knew we would survive. Or maybe he didn't, and we just got lucky.

Aella isn't like Earth's moon. I'm grateful because it would have sucked to hang out in a crater while we figured out our next move. The mountain we end up on is mostly stone, but I see a few trees and some sort of moss. Either way, it's infinitely better than the Garden.

After setting me gently down, X shakes a little bit, trying to shift back into his human form. I turn around to give him some privacy. When I feel a change in the air, I turn back. My eyes bug out of my head when I see he's naked.

"Oh my gosh!" I squeak and whirl back around.

"Sorry," he grumbles. "I lost my clothes when I shifted."

"Well… maybe we can make some? Like, I don't know…out of leaves?"

He hums a bit, then goes silent. I wait for a few minutes.

"I think I figured it out. Turn around."

"Oh!" I exclaim. "How did you do that?" Somehow, he's wearing pants made of black scales.

He shrugs. "No idea. I just had a feeling I could do it."

"Huh. I guess it's something your people can do, then?"

"I guess so," he says quietly.

I walk closer to him. We're only one foot apart now. "What's this?"

"What?"

I point to something on his forehead that I've never noticed before since we've only seen each other in the dark.

He laughs. "I can't see it, Addison Rose. I've never really seen myself before. Describe it to me."

"It's a jewel, kind of. In the middle of your forehead. It's small. Shaped like a diamond. It's the color of warm caramel, the same as your eyes. It's beautiful."

I lean forward and touch it with my thumb. He puts his hand over mine. I clear my throat.

"Thanks for saving me." I smile. "You were pretty badass. A dragon, huh?"

He smiles. "I guess so."

I frown. "All those other people, though... they're still trapped there in those glass boxes. It's awful. We need to help them, X."

He picks my hand up and turns it around in his, again and again. His eyes are full of wonder as he strokes my hand. I'm not surprised. The only touches he's experienced in his life have been for death and pain. I'm happy to give him something else. Just between us.

"Yes, Addison Rose, I think we do."

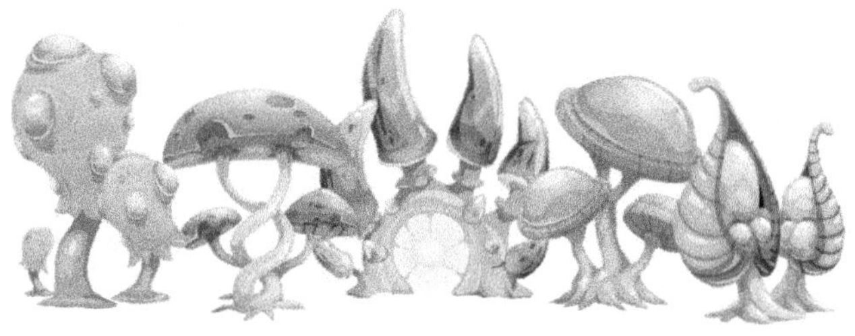

Tending the garden of the house she inherited, Elizabeth Knollston feels connected to the generations who came before her through the rose bushes and perennials planted by other hands. More than just lilies have taken root in her garden plot.

Little wonder then that family plays such an important part in her story, which she dedicates to her dad, mom, and uncle.

THE THREE TRELLISES

Elizabeth Knollston

"Do something for others if you can. No matter how small, it makes a difference."

– Douglas Ray Johnson

IN THE YARD ACROSS THE dusty dirt road, the rays of the late afternoon sun caught on trinkets hanging from the branches of a thick oak tree. The majority of its limbs stretched into clusters of foliage, the sunlight crafting pockets of bright crisp leaves, intertwined with deep shadows of dark green. Tucked into the shadows were limbs devoid of life, bark dry and rough where death and decay had crept in.

Harold Anderson, a high school math teacher two years away from retirement, sat in his rental car, and fussed with his tie as he stared out across the road at the beat-up old farmhouse.

The farm had seen better days. The picket fence was more bare wood than white paint, with several pickets half-broken or missing altogether. Volunteer trees clustered along the fence line, and dandelions choked out most of the grass. Parked in front of the house was a rusted-out Ford pickup truck and laying under its shade was a dog.

Harold glanced at his reflection in the rear-view mirror. A man he didn't recognize stared back at him with sallow skin, eyes devoid of their bright zest. Thick locks of amber hair had turned to thin, fragile gray strands, now cut short due to necessity.

This was a stupid idea.

The key was still in the ignition. He reached out and grabbed it. The metal head of the key bit into the flesh of his thumb as his eyes fell on the photo. On a whim, he'd taken it from his wallet and clipped it to an air vent right before he'd left the rental car lot.

In the photo, his kids were small, his wife unencumbered with the burden of caring for her husband, and Harold looked fit and healthy. His eldest daughter, Mary, had tucked the photo into one of her monthly encouragement cards after his diagnosis with stage two lung cancer.

The diagnosis had been a punch to the gut. He'd never smoked, neither did his immediate family. The few colleagues at the school who smoked were courteous and followed school and state policies, never smoking around him. Harold's new-found health crisis baffled his doctors; a mystery he cursed many times over.

At first the oncologist was optimistic. There were options and treatments to knock back the cancer. Harold did the chemo, endured it in the belief it'd do its job. It hadn't. The chemo weakened, not only his body but his mind as well.

Anger and grief over being robbed of time with his loved ones, of finishing his forty-three-year career, a weakened shell of who he used to be, drove him over the edge. Withdrawing into himself, the dark crept into his thoughts.

It'd been Anne, his middle daughter, and her fiancé, Tim, who stuck with him during that time. After a few months of gentle coaxing, Tim, an associate pastor, convinced Howard to attend a support group for individuals with cancer at the local Methodist church.

The first few times, he'd been sullen and withdrawn. But over time he opened up and took comfort in the shared experiences with those in the group. He began to hope again.

Until the cancer had spread into the lymph nodes in his lungs.

Sharon, the woman who led the group, noticed the change in Harold's demeanor, took him aside, and talked with him. A few meetings after their initial private conversation, she introduced the idea of an alternative treatment outside the accepted realm of Western medicine.

His hand slipped off the key and moved to pick up the crumpled piece of paper on the passenger's seat. In Sharon's tidy cursive writing was an address for a rundown old farm in northern Iowa. No number, no contact information. Sharon had whispered that this treatment wasn't for most people. In fact, she could only share it with a select few. But she'd experienced it herself, and she felt Harold would be an excellent match for it.

What a joke, was his initial response. But it'd been the desire to watch his grandkids grow, to walk Anne down the aisle, and to celebrate with Harry, his youngest, as he graduated from law school in a little over a year and a half, that drove him to make a decision. To take a chance.

He didn't want to be a burden to Betsy, as she drove him to appointments, cared for him on the rough days, and silently cried in the bathroom on the good days. If something out there could knock the cancer back, he was going to try it.

The joke had turned into a plan, and the plan turned into action, which saw him staring at the rundown farmhouse, wondering what in the world he'd gotten himself into.

Checking his tie in the mirror one last time, he ran a hand through his thinning hair and got out of the car. Habits died hard as he checked both ways, despite there'd been no traffic while he'd been sitting in the car.

As he passed by the old Ford truck, he paused, unsure about the dog. It raised its head, snout lifted to sniff the air, huffed and went back to sleep.

Cracked concrete steps led to the front door. He reached out for the iron guard rail, his body faltering more than he liked, and felt the railing shift beneath his weight.

"Not very useful anymore, are you?" he muttered.

The screen door groaned as he opened it to rap on the door beneath it, a solid piece of wood. With no window to see inside, and no immediate response, he knocked again, impatient.

Still no response. He let the screen door bang against the frame. Retracing his steps, he decided to follow the sidewalk around the house. As he rounded the corner, a gust of wind greeted him, scented with the sweet perfume of flowering plants. He couldn't help but sneeze.

"Allergies?"

Harold pulled out a handkerchief, sneezed again and then coughed. "No, not really."

Stretched out alongside the house, were two rows of fruit trees. A woman was crouched down, working at the base of one of the trees. Light danced with shadow through the branches, and played tricks with Harold's vision as he watched her get to her feet.

Her movements were slow and deliberate as if her body had seen better days, but as she turned, her face was smooth with not a blemish to be found. An initial assessment described a woman with graying hair and a frail body. But as the woman moved out of the shadows, Harold saw a robust young person with bright red hair walking towards him.

"Hi, I'm Ginger." She extended a hand, noticed the gardening glove, and laughed as she removed it. Extending her hand again, she said, "Sharon called and let me know you'd be stopping by."

"It's a pleasure to meet you." Harold hesitated but didn't want to appear rude, so he took her hand and was pleased with the firm handshake. "I'm Harold Anderson. I don't know if Sharon told you much about my situation. I'm not sure-"

"I'm going to stop you right there, Mr. Anderson." Ginger turned to put her trowel and gloves on a bench tucked up against the house. "I know this place doesn't look like much, but I can assure you, that if you're willing, it has a lot to offer."

Harold frowned at her turn of phrase.

Ginger smiled. "You are ill, yes?"

He nodded.

"And Sharon believed you'd be a good match for the treatment I can offer, right?"

He nodded again.

"Let me give you the tour. Tour first, then we'll discuss terms, and if you want, we'll talk about how it all works."

What else could he say? First impression of the place told him he doubted he'd take her up on whatever she offered. But what would it hurt to do the tour and hear her out? He'd traveled over a thousand miles to see this place, to find out if it could help him. He could admit he was at least curious.

Harold listened to Ginger as they walked along the side of the house and through the row of fruit trees.

"Inherited this place from my mom, and her mom before her. Goes back a couple generations. Before, we came over from the Old Country. You know how it is I'm sure, families seeking a better life and all that. It's seen better days, I know, but it keeps me going and does the job."

Ginger led him towards the barn. The one building on the property which had been kept up. The siding boasted a traditional fresh, bright red color, with a crisp white trim. It was the quintessential barn, at least on the outside.

The barn's interior had been completely gutted and repurposed. Sections of the roof been replaced with panels to allow for generous amounts of light to fill the barn, and on one side, a row of windows had also been installed. The barn had been turned into a greenhouse.

They moved through the elaborate maze of raised beds, Harold's head swinging back and forth to look at the variety of plants. He had a passing knowledge of basic backyard gardens, after years of helping Betsy with her hobby. She'd be in heaven if she were here, he thought.

"Harold?"

He realized Ginger had been naming plants, but he hadn't heard anything she'd been saying.

"I'm sorry, I guess I'm just a little–," he struggled to find the right word.

"Overwhelmed? Underwhelmed?" Ginger asked with a kind smile. "It's okay. People who come to see me don't know what to expect."

He found a small measure of relief in her words and returned her smile, still not sure what he could say. He certainly hadn't known what to expect, and he would have never had guessed any of this.

"I guess you could say a green thumb runs in the family," Ginger laughed as she continued to walk them through the barn and out the other side. "That's a small part of what makes this all work."

A little way off from the barn were three trellises. Their metal frames bent at odd angles and weeds clung to the base of each one. Where the barn boasted well-maintained, raised garden beds, it was obvious these were forgotten.

"Would you like some tea? It's fresh," Ginger offered.

The tour had been a gracious gesture, but it was tempting to just thank the woman and leave. There was nothing here, which gave him confidence Ginger could provide something to help with his cancer. But he found he couldn't leave. Not yet, at least. Besides, following her around the farm had winded him, taking a moment to catch his breath wouldn't hurt.

"Sure, that would be great. Thanks."

Ginger once again led the way, walking around the barn and back towards the house. She motioned for him to sit in one of the lawn chairs while she stepped inside for the tea. It didn't take her long, and as Harold sipped on the refreshing mint flavored beverage, his shoulders dropped, tension draining from his body.

"Tell me about your family," Ginger asked as she sat down across from him with her own glass.

Harold cupped the glass in his hands and stared into the amber liquid before telling his life story to a woman he'd only met a little over twenty minutes ago. The words poured out of him. It felt natural to paint a vivid picture of his time teaching, building a family with his wife, and the pride he felt about his three children.

"And then I was diagnosed with lung cancer. It was like someone was trying to play a joke on me, and then when it all sunk in, I...I was angry at first. Why did this have to happen to me? What had I done to deserve this? I never smoked, seldom drank, and did the best I could with my health. I've got a great family. I want to be there for my children and their grandchildren. But now, it's just all being taken away from me. The chemo treatments just aren't working, and I...hate them." The last words came out with a vengeance that startled him.

It was true.

He hated going to chemo.

He'd initially gone because the doctors had assured him of beating the cancer back. Betsy and their children wanted him to fight. But the chemo hadn't eaten away at the cancer, it'd eaten away at his physical strength, his mental acuity. It felt like he was drifting in a fog for days after treatment, not to mention the nausea, diarrhea, and pain it caused.

But he was a fighter. He wanted to have more time for his family. That was why he'd come here after all.

He stopped talking, and looked over at Ginger, tears glistened on her cheeks and her eyes shown with understanding.

"Harold. Sharon was right to send you to me. I do think I may be able to help you." She stood, went inside and returned with a stack of papers. "I know this is not going to make much sense, and may even seem a little shady. But before I can explain what I do, I need you to read through these and sign them. It's mainly a lot of nondisclosure agreements and legalities I need taken care of before I can help you."

As a high school teacher, Harold didn't have too much to do with the legal world. When Harry announced his decision to go into law, Harold read what he could to keep up when his son visited. So, he felt a small measure of security as he leafed through the papers.

He agreed with Ginger's word of warning at the oddity of signing so many non-disclosures. On the other hand, if she truly had some form of miracle drug, refined through years of hard work on her part, she'd hardly want a pharmaceutical company to steal her intellectual property.

He handed the signed stack of papers back to her, and watched as Ginger thumbed through each one. When she laid the last of the papers down, she turned to him and smiled.

"Welcome, Harold. Thank you for seeking me out at this difficult time in your life. What I'm going to share with you won't seem possible or even plausible. But I assure you it is, and if you're successful, it might turn out to be exactly what you're looking for."

Harold's hand ran down the length of his tie. Her choice of words wasn't what he'd expected.

"Walk with me."

A Most Unusual Garden

They moved back through the barn and out towards the three forgotten trellises.

"Do you know the saying, you put your blood, sweat and tears into something?"

"Yes."

"Good. What I'm able to do, builds upon that concept. Literally, actually. I'll collect your literal blood, sweat, and tears, use their essence to bond it with the plants I'll select to create a treatment for your cancer. I'm essentially tailor-making a medicine that will be born of you, bound to you, and thus be a much more potent medicine for you to take."

A wave of foolishness washed over him. This was a hoax, it had to be. What she was talking about was impossible. This wasn't science, it was magic. A myth. Something to be found in fairy tales and fables.

He needed to politely excuse himself, to forget this misbegotten adventure.

But Ginger stepped up to a trellis, stretched out her hand, and touched the top of the tallest weed.

Harold watched in disbelief as the weed transformed. It's thick stalk, coated in thin spines, changed into chunky thorns, its rounded leaves grew fat and jagged, delicate buds appeared and then blossomed into exquisite white roses. It stretched and grew, twisting through the wire frame, until the metal vanished under an abundance of fresh life.

"How?"

"The how doesn't matter. Right now, the only thing that matters is that you can believe."

Ginger moved back to his side and pointed at the trellises. "Each trellis is a gateway to one of three worlds. The first is considered the Upper World. The second will take you to the Middle World, and the third goes to what can be considered as the Under World. You must travel to each of these places, and a task will be set before you. Once a task is complete, you will return to me and I will collect either your blood, sweat or tears."

"I don't—"

Ginger turned, her gaze sharp and intent. "I know. It's difficult for the human brain to make sense of the vastness of our world. But there is so much more to it than one person can ever understand in their lifetime. Know this, at any time, you can leave. All I ask is you remember to keep to our agreement. You can't talk about this to anyone. Not your family, your friends, or even Sharon. But the choice is yours. I can't guarantee that what you go through will produce the solution your body needs, but it will at least help ease the pain."

Harold listened to her. He heard the words but could only see how crazy the whole thing sounded. What am I doing? What is this woman really up to? Was Sharon in on some kind of scam?

Despite the alarms going off inside his mind, Harold found the word slipping from his lips. "Okay."

Ginger pointed to the newly transformed trellis. "The first step then, is to travel to the Upper World, all you have to do is pass through the trellis."

Harold eyed the structure, noting the same scenery through its arch and beyond it on both sides. He'd step through it and when nothing happened, he'd just leave. Get in the car, drive back to his hotel and then fly home.

Adjusting his tie, Harold cleared his throat, stepped up to the trellis, and then stepped through.

A Most Unusual Garden

Words of rebuke were on the tip of his tongue when he blinked and whirled around.

The trellis was gone.

The barn was gone.

Ginger was gone.

All he saw before him was rolling hills of luscious green grasses, their frayed tops swaying in the breeze. Sunlight cast its warm, golden summer glow across the land, and the call of birds filled the air.

"This isn't possible," Harold muttered.

He took a few steps back and then a few steps forward. Nothing happened.

"No...no, no no." He waved his hands in the air, called out for help, and pinched himself a few times. Everything remained the same.

Panic crept in around the edges of his disbelief. Harold walked forward, the hills stretching on in an endless sea before him. He veered off to the right, picking up the pace, and crested one of the bigger hills. In different circumstances, the view should have taken his breath away.

The gently rolling hills gave way to a stretch of sandy beach, caressing a sea of crystal blue water. Suspended above the water appeared to be a crystal city. Its exterior walls reflected the sun's light, casting sun dogs out to dance in the sky. Thick walls gave way to tall, delicate spindles, their points piercing the milky clouds floating through the clear blue sky.

Clinging to a thin veneer of reason, Harold headed off towards the crystal city. If there was going to be anyone in this impossible place, it would be there.

As he drew closer though, the blue skies darkened to a milky gray, the clouds expanded, growing heavy with the threat of rain. The once pristine beach took on an ominous look as thick, curling brambles replaced the sparkling sand.

Harold slowed his pace and stopped at the base of the last hill, searching for a way across the treacherous landscape to the city. A gust of wind ripped through him, its chill wrapping itself around his body. Riding the back of the air was a whimper. A small voice, crying out into the building fury of the storm clouds.

He held still, listening for the pitiful sound to come again.

Another gust of wind pushed against him, and it forced him to raise his arm, shielding his face from the dirt and debris. He turned his head to the side, trying to hide from the worst of it, and saw the storm wasn't extending its anger past the stretch of brambles.

Harold turned from the storm and moved through the waist high grass.

What am I doing? This is crazy, he thought as he turned back to the blackened skies, the sea water stirring in agitation, waves cresting with white caps.

She's drugged me. That's all this can be. There'd been something in the tea, some kind of hallucinogenic or mind-altering drug. Who knew what she grew on that farm? It would explain the nondisclosure forms. What a fool to fall for such a trap. Maybe it was some kind of exhortation ring. They preyed upon the vulnerable with offers of help, but in reality, put them in embarrassing situations to use as blackmail.

All I need to do is wake up. To just ride this torment out. When I get out of this, I'll go to the cops and pray my family can forgive my stupidity.

Harold stopped walking and stood still, refusing to play into the delusion any longer. He thought of Mary and her techniques to help calm her body and mind when faced with overwhelming anxiety. He took a deep breath in, held it, and then slowly exhaled. As his body relaxed, he closed his eyes and pictured his family, each one hugging him in understanding as he explained why he'd gotten tangled up in such a silly and foolish adventure.

The cry for help refused to be ignored. His eyes opened and he turned towards the sound. Whatever or whoever was crying for help sounded as if they were becoming increasingly more desperate. A childish impulse overtook him, and he clapped his hands over his ears, trying to muffle the pitiful cry of distress. It's just a hallucination. It's just a hallucination. It isn't real.

The cry for help wouldn't be dissuaded, wrapping its pitiful sound around him, refusing to let go.

Can I really walk away from someone who might need help? Even if this was some grand hallucination brought on by who knows what Ginger put in my tea?

He'd always helped those in need, neighbors, his community, kids in trouble at school, and his family. It was at the core of who he was. He gave of his time, his strength and his friendship to those around him. It was something the cancer stole from him, weakening his body and dulling his mind.

Disgust and anger surged inside of him, and he screamed and screamed and screamed.

His body had betrayed him. Made him weak, vulnerable. It took all his strength to teach, even with the school system working with him and bringing in a substitute teacher to cover his bad days after chemo. But it meant no after-school activities, no going to the games and cheering on the athletes, sitting in the auditorium and watching the band or school musicals. The cancer had forced his days of volunteering with the local clubs to taper down to almost nothing, and the calls, asking for his help, had stopped.

Perhaps the worst was the pity and distancing from those around him. He knew they thought they were doing him a favor, letting him rest, have some peace, but it only tormented him to know he'd once been a part of something larger than himself, and now all he could do was sit at home and pretend not to hear the fear in his wife's voice.

Did he really care if this was all a hallucination? What did it matter?

For the first time in over a year he was jogging, moving as if he was thirty years younger. Fit and healthy. It'd felt good, even if it was only in a dream.

Harold abruptly decided he didn't care. If someone needed help, he'd help them.

Spinning around, he ran towards the cries for help. His back now to the crystal city, he jogged along the edge of the beach. The cries were becoming louder, and when the city was just a dull gleam in the distance, he came across the source of distress.

In the middle of the bramble encrusted beach appeared to be a young woman. The menacing thorns of the brambles snagged her faded, yellow sun dress. Even from his vantage point, he could see where the razor-sharp edges cut into her legs and arms.

"Hang on ma'am, I'm coming to help."

The woman turned at the sound of his voice, her auburn hair whipping around in the wind, obscuring her face.

"No, don't! If you come out here, you'll only get caught too." The woman called back.

Harold could hear the brokenness in her voice, the desperation.

"I just didn't want to be alone. The storm is coming, and I just didn't want to be alone."

The woman's body quivered and to Harold's horror, she collapsed. Bright, red blood soaked into the dress as the brambles claimed her body.

Feeling desperate, Harold looked around for some way to gain safer access to the woman. But there were no paths cut into the brambles. It was a solid carpet of nightmarish thorns. The patent leather shoes and slacks were no match against the treacherous beach. But he had to try.

He stepped forward and grimaced as the thorns cut through the soles of his shoes. After only a few steps, the pain drove him back to the safety of the soft, welcoming grass. Desperate, he watched as the woman's chest slowed in its rise and fall. She would have lost a lot of blood by now, he reasoned, and he was sure she'd exhausted herself trying to get out of the tangled mess.

What was his life worth? He'd already endured so much; he could endure a little more. With a deep breath, jaw set, Harold stepped forward again and then again. Ignoring the pain of the thorns piercing his feet, ripping through his slacks to pierce his legs, he continued until he reached the woman.

He bent over, his flesh ripped open as he reached down to slip his arms around the woman. Energy and strength drained from his body with each slice and prick from the thorns, and he prayed he'd have enough to lift and carry the woman to safety.

The brutal onslaught of the pain slowed his progress, but with grim determination he made his way back to the edge of the hills. As he stepped on the soft, warm grass, his body trembled, and he laid the woman down as carefully as he could, and then collapsed next to her.

His shoes were in tatters, his feet and lower legs a bloody mess. Tears slid down his cheeks as a thorn pierced his skin, fire blossoming. He turned to the woman and shook her shoulder. "Ma'am? Ma'am, can you hear me?"

The woman was still breathing and when she groaned, Harold let himself fall back against the grass, the warmth of the sun spreading across his body. His mind spun to the next problem. Where was he going to find anything to treat not only his wounds, but hers as well?

When he opened his eyes, he sat up and looked around. The raging storm, the angry thicket of brambles, vanished. The cheerful exterior of Ginger's barn was only a few feet away from him.

"What did you do to me?" he demanded, eyeing Ginger as she got up from a chair and walked over to him.

"It was your choice to travel through the gate."

Harold shook his head. "You drugged me, didn't you?"

Ginger gave him a soft smile and knelt beside him. "No. You've experienced the impossible." She gestured towards his arms, legs, and feet. "May I?"

Harold eyed her with suspicion and then looked down to where she was pointing. His shoes were in pieces, his legs and feet bloody, and his arms held deep scratches. "No, that can't be. How can that–?" He twisted around to stare at the trellis.

"You must accept what you cannot if you wish to continue."

Ginger gently took off what remained of his shoes and pulled back his pant legs to treat his wounds. "This is the first of what I need. I will collect some of your blood."

Harold could only stare at the woman as she worked to treat his injuries.

"I have a pair of pants and shoes you should be able to wear. Would you like them? The Middle World awaits you."

Could it have been real? Surely Ginger wouldn't have inflicted such horrible wounds, just to try to make him believe? That possibility was too much, and Harold decided it was simpler to believe.

"I'll try them."

"Good. Sit here for a minute, and let the paste soak in. It'll help take the bite out of those nasty cuts."

Harold let his body flop back against the earth. What had he gotten himself into? Something far beyond his understanding or comprehension. He believed there were mysteries in the universe to which man wasn't meant to understand. Perhaps he'd stumbled into one of them.

"Here." Ginger handed him the pants and shoes, then turned to provide him a moment of privacy. "You'll next need to pass into the Middle World."

"Thank you," he said, taking the clothes.

Ginger turned back around and gave him an approving look. "They're a good fit. Excellent."

She walked over to the middle trellis and touched the weeds, which had claimed it as their own. Instead of roses, thick, twisting vines sprouted from the ground, weaving their way back and forth through the latticework of the trellis's sides. Broad, brightly stripped leaves uncurled, and the heady scent of earth, pregnant with freshly fallen rain, filled the air.

Harold watched Ginger step to the side. It was time to make a decision. Against reason, he chose the impossible and walked through the next trellis.

Humidity attacked, and it instantly drenched him in sweat. Strands of sunlight filtered down through the thick forest foliage. He pushed branches out of the way, trying to take stock of where the trellis had transported him. He spied a narrow, almost indiscernible trail, winding its way through the giant trees, thick bushes, and ground cover, all fighting for their right to survive.

With no other way to go, Harold followed the path. It gradually widened, until it was evidently a well-traveled path, with deep ruts dug into the earth. The humidity grew worse as he traveled. But despite its oppressive presence, Harold enjoyed the music of the forest. Birds called back and forth, and somewhere in the distance he could hear water as it rushed through the channel it'd carved into the earth.

Harold lifted a particularly heavy branch, laden with clusters of bright orange fruit.

"Ahh, good day to you sir."

A few yards ahead of Harold was a middle-aged man with a welcoming grin.

"It looks as though you've been traveling for some time," the man commented, eyeing Harold's sweat soaked shirt and hair plastered to his face. "Would you care for a ride? I can take you to the next village."

The offer couldn't have come at a better time. Harold was beginning to succumb to the unbearable humidity. The man had a small cart with a tarp covering his goods. There was just enough room for someone to sit on the end.

"That would be wonderful, thank you," Harold said as he sat down, glad to give his body a rest. "I'm Harold, it's a pleasure to meet you."

"Well met, sir. My name is Shivar. Tradesmen by day and storyteller by night." The man hefted a thick leather strap over his shoulder and began to continue on his way.

Harold turned, resting his back against the side of the cart, his legs propped up over whatever Shivar had tucked away in the wagon. The man was jovial and lighthearted, telling Harold about his family, the different goods he traded amongst the villages, and how he'd inherited the honor of telling his people's stories.

As the cart rocked back and forth, Harold's mind began to wander, turning to thoughts of what would happen in this place. Ginger said he'd encounter a task in each of the three worlds. It was obvious his first task had been to free the woman from the brambles.

As time went on, he took in the scenery, the craftsmanship of the cart and the man pulling him along. He realized Shivar moved with an unusual gait. There wasn't the usual, rhythmic swing to his body as a person would have when walking, even under the burden of pulling a wagon. Shivar's body shifted to the left, leaned forward and then bobbed to the right.

"Shivar, are you alright?" Harold felt compelled to ask.

Shivar came to a stop and wiped his brow. "It's nothing I haven't had since a child."

Guilt rose up like bile stinging his throat at the realization his weight added to the man's burden. Harold got out and walked up to the front of the cart.

Shivar leaned forward and patted his right leg. "A mild discomfort on the good days, an annoyance on the bad. My boy usually helps me with these trips, but his young wife is with child and nearing the day of birthing."

Harold's face went red. "I'm sorry, I didn't know. Here, let me help you."

"Oh, no, it's no trouble at all, I'm always glad to have the company and an ear to listen to my stories."

Harold wouldn't take no for an answer. After a few minutes of back and forth, Shivar climbed up into the wagon and Harold slipped the strap over his head and pulled.

It was difficult to find a rhythm, but in time, he discovered the wagon wasn't as taxing as he'd feared. His heart felt glad at being able to be the one to shoulder the burden and provide Shivar a time to rest and relax.

Stories of Shivar's life drifted into silence, and Harold glanced back to see the man had fallen asleep. As Harold continued through the forest, his thoughts turned to his wife.

He imagined Betsy sitting in the back of the wagon, relaxing and enjoying the beauty of the world around her. At first, as he did so, each step was a struggle, and he felt a sourness boil inside of him.

He felt guilt for becoming a burden in their golden years. The time when so many of their friends were retiring, going on extended vacations, or setting up vacation homes in Florida or Arizona. Betsy always dreamed of the time when they'd be able to travel to various National Parks in a RV and stay for a few weeks, taking in the sights and hiking each day.

With the cancer not responding to the chemo treatments, they'd discussed the hard conversations they'd hoped would have been several years in the future. He'd wanted to give Betsy her dream of traveling across the country. She'd sacrificed so much for him throughout the years, volunteering at the school, helping him with the endless projects a teacher had on top of their regular duties. She'd hardly ever complained as he'd sat at their dining room table, papers scattered as he'd graded tests, essays and assignments. She'd joined him in all the games, sitting there and rooting for the students right along with him.

Then he thought of Shivar, who'd gladly let Harold ride in the wagon, despite the trouble with his leg. He'd happily shouldered the extra weight, and had felt joy despite the pain. Harold realized he could hold the same attitude.

It didn't mean he'd find the physical strength each day to move, maybe not even be able to get out of bed, but he could work on finding the mental strength, of finding joy even through the pain. If there was one way he could lessen Betsy's burden, it would be to laugh, to share and to explore what they could in the time they had left. He didn't want to leave the last of her memories as a man who'd withdrawn into himself. He wanted her to remember him as he'd always been. Loving, grateful and full of good humor.

"Thank you, my friend."

Harold jumped as he hadn't realized Shivar had gotten out of the wagon and moved up to keep pace with him.

Harold came to a stop as Shivar extended his hand. Harold took it and grinned back at the man as they firmly shook hands.

When he blinked, he was back in front of the barn.

"Would you like some water?"

Harold nodded and gladly took the glass Ginger offered.

"I must collect some of your sweat."

She patiently waited as he took a few deep drinks of the cool, refreshing water and then stepped forward and wiped his forehead with a deep blue handkerchief.

"I would advise you to rest for a few minutes before you travel to the Under World. Of the three it will be the most difficult."

Harold didn't need to be told twice. The combination of the humidity and the weight of the cart had leeched away most of his strength. He sunk down into one of the plastic chairs and finished the glass of water. In companionable silence, Ginger took the glass and refilled it. He felt weary, but not weighted down. If he had to describe it, he would have said it was as if he'd been shouldering an unbearable weight for months, and for the first time he felt as if he'd been freed.

As he finished the second glass of water, Ginger walked to the third trellis, and when she touched its cluster of weeds, they shriveled into dark, brown clumps of decay. Fog lifted from the ground and sank its teeth into the air around the trellis.

"When you're ready."

Harold sat the glass down on the ground, stood, and stretched. He eyed the third trellis. Snatches of myths, legends and fables sprang to mind as he thought about the Under World and Ginger's warning. He wondered what he would meet there as he walked over to it and stepped through the fog.

The world he entered was bathed in the soft glow of the moon, its orb suspended just above the horizon. It was a clear night, the sky radiant with the light of thousands of stars, and the milky way was stretched across it in all its glory. The air was warm and scented with the hint of honeysuckle and lavender.

He looked to his right, noting this world was an unending expanse of desert, cacti standing as silent guardians of the land. But it was the view to his left, which took his breath away.

Stretched across the expanse of earth to sky was the largest tree he'd ever beheld. A behemoth of ancient life. Its trunk was wide enough to encircle a large city, with its branches darkening the sky. He couldn't help but be drawn to the imposing tree, and as he drew closer, he realized it looked as if someone had excavated the earth from around it, leaving an impossible tangle of roots exposed.

The thick roots, larger still than any living tree Harold had ever seen, twisted and turned on each other, crafting tunnels and hidden spaces all cloaked in inky blackness. A shiver of fear ran through Harold, and he wondered if he should turn and walk away. There was nothing else to go towards.

In the Upper World he'd been drawn to the city, in the Middle World a path had been laid out before him. Now, in the Under World, this was the only object he could see which might hold the task he was meant to accomplish.

He'd never been one for the nighttime. His eldest daughter, Mary, had always preferred the night to the day. She'd done some of her best schoolwork late at night; when the world was sleeping, she'd come alive. Some of his fondest memories were taking her outside when dusk was settling and she'd run back and forth in delight, trying to catch fireflies.

Harold wished she was here with him. She would have taken his hand and led the way to the tree with unbridled excitement and curiosity.

But Harold had come this far through the impossible. He wasn't going to stop just because this wasn't his preferred time of day. He continued walking towards the tree, and as he began to come under its canopy, he could feel the temperature drop. When he finally reached the roots, he was shivering.

The night was silent. There was no breeze, no sounds of waves crashing against a beach, no delightful bird song to float around him, only silence and the inky blackness surrounding the roots.

Harold took a step forward, the darkness under the roots almost impossible to see through. His heart began to pound as he wondered what might be hiding in the dark. He stumbled and reached out to catch himself, his hand brushing up against one of the mighty roots.

The darkened space crafted underneath the root lit up with a soft white light. Harold couldn't help but stumble back a few steps at the abrupt change. As soon as his hand left the root, the light faded. Curiosity replaced fear, and he stepped forward and touched the root again. The soft, white light returned. He took a tentative step underneath the root and looked around.

It was not as he expected.

Harold stood in the middle of his living room.

For a moment he wondered if he'd failed, or if he'd dreamed the entire experience, from the flight up to Des Moines, to meeting the red-haired woman, to believing in what was impossible.

As he looked around, he realized things were not quite right. Books which were normally stacked on the end tables and coffee table had been cleared. Extra chairs had been scattered through the living room, and as he leaned back to look in the dining room, he saw a table, fully extended and laden with food. His stomach rumbled.

He walked over to the table, noting it was full of his favorite foods. Miniature pigs in a blanket, apple crumble pie, loaded nachos, green and black olives, and so much more. He couldn't help himself and reached out to snag a few pigs in the blanket, but his hand passed right through the food.

He frowned. That was disappointing.

The front door opened, and voices drifted in. Harold moved back into the living room and watched as his wife, two daughters and son walked into the house, clothed in black. His frown deepened.

Anne wrapped her arms around her mom and was whispering something in her ear as Mary rubbed their mom's back. Harry turned back to the door and greeted Tom and Sarah, their next-door neighbors.

"We put the food out about ten minutes ago. I hope that's alright," Sarah asked Harry, faced creased with concern.

"That works. We really appreciate you helping with this."

"How could we not?" Sarah replied, wrapping her arms around Harry in a tight hug. "Your father meant so much to us."

Harold shook his head. No, he thought. I refuse to see this. He moved back to the spot in the living room where he'd first appeared, turned around and took a step. Nothing happened except unexpectedly moving through Betsy as she made her way to the dining room.

"No," Harold said out loud.

He moved through the living room, reaching out and touching everything, the walls, the fireplace, the chairs, anything that might feel like the rough bark of the tree's roots. But with everything he touched, his hand simply passed through.

So Harold did the only thing he could think of. He walked out the front door, down the steps and marched down the street, away from his house, from the family mourning the loss of their loved one.

Time escaped him as he kept his gaze down, focused on the sidewalk. Step after step, he forced himself to move away from the fate he refused to acknowledge. Knowing it and having to see it were two different things.

What kind of task was that? What could he accomplish having to see the misery and pain his wife and children would endure? The grief they'd carry with them for the rest of their lives.

Harold vividly remembered the night his own father had passed away.

Timothy Anderson had been eighty-three and had suffered a massive heart attack. It'd happened suddenly. No warnings and nothing a medical team could have done. Even though his father had lived a long and good life, the abrupt departure of his death had shaken Harold. It'd left him feeling empty and afraid. Afraid of his own mortality, of the hidden mistakes in his body which might spring forth and claim his own life. Then his fears had come true. They had diagnosed him with cancer.

Grief was something which never left a person. There were still moments which would overwhelm Harold as he caught snippets of a song, or came across something which reminded him of the days his father spent in the woodworking shop. The memories would flood him and Harold would go off and find a space to shed his tears.

With the diagnosis of cancer, Harold was tortured by the haunted looks he'd catch upon his family's faces, the knowledge that their time together was limited. Death was a natural extension of life, but when you knew death was standing on your doorstep, its long cold reach touching your life, it changed things. Your mind dwells on the darker "what ifs" and "is this my last moment", instead of the bright optimism life brings with each new day.

Harold stopped, looked up and growled. He was right back where he'd started. He turned and began walking in the opposite direction, but stumbled as his foot hit the bottom of his porch in only a few steps.

He turned again, and this time ran away, but with each direction he turned, he was only running towards his house and not away from it. Fury exploded out of him. "I don't want this!"

Nothing changed.

Exhausted and empty Harold stopped at the bottom of the steps, staring up into the big front windows. Inside, people were moving around, hugging each other and eating the foods his neighbors had prepared for his family.

He watched Anne, holding a scrapbook, walk up to one of the ladies from his support group. She opened it, slowly flipping through the pictures and then she laughed. Harold was taken a back. She turned another page and laughed again, and then Mary walked over, glanced at the scrapbook and she too joined in the laughter. Curious as to what it was about, Harold moved up to the porch. But all he could see were their faces bright with joy and their shoulders moving up and down as their laughter turned into a fit of giggles.

A need to know passed through him, and so he went inside.

"And then Dad got out of the car, took off his hat and began flapping it around." He caught the end of Mary's story, and as he looked over Anne's shoulder he saw the picture was one from a family vacation. He couldn't help but smile. He remembered that trip, it'd been one of his girls' favorite trips to reminisce over. Nothing had seemed to go right, but he and Betsy had somehow managed to pull it off with everyone returning home in one piece.

The deep rumble of Harry's laughter caught his attention, and Harold turned, moving through the house until he saw him handing Betsy a roll of paper towels.

"You know your dad wouldn't want us to go to too much trouble fussing after him," Betsy said, her voice soft and filled with an emotion that punched Harold in the gut.

"Maybe," Harry shrugged, "but he was a great guy. Not just as a dad, but a person in this community. I don't think he'd want us sitting around feeling sorry for ourselves. We remember him through celebrating his life, the good and the bad." Harry reached out and pulled his mom in for a hug. "We'll cry, but we'll laugh. We'll smile, and we'll remember everything he did for us. And we'll take that with us and pass it on."

Harold watched as Betsy pulled away, tears streaming down her cheeks. "When did my little boy become such a wise man?"

Harold had to turn away, the emotions flooding him were overwhelming. He looked around the room at Mary, Anne, his neighbors, fellow teachers, former students, and then turned back to watch Harry and Betsy.

He began to cry, and then he began to smile through the tears, as he realized they weren't tears of sorrow or self-pity. They were tears of joy. Joy and love for his children, his wife and the community he'd been fortunate to be a part of. He'd lived his life with everything he had, and he knew there wasn't a thing he'd change about it.

When he returned, got home from his journey, he'd work hard to create fresh memories, times filled with laughter and joy. Moments and experiences for his wife and children to look back on and smile. He didn't want the last of his life to be full of sorrow, for those he loved to carry dark, bleak days around inside them. Instead, he wanted to fill them with light and love.

"Harold." Ginger's voice called to him, soft yet firm. "I must collect your tears before they dry."

Harold could only nod, his emotions still gripped in the revelations from his time in the Under World. Ginger wiped his face with a delicate piece of muslin.

"Would you like a moment to sit?"

Harold was tempted, but there was an energy coursing through him he hadn't felt in a long time. He shook his head. "No, thank you."

"Would you like to see what you came here for?"

A Most Unusual Garden

He gave her a puzzled look. "I thought I just did."

Ginger gave him a kind smile. "Come on."

They walked inside the barn, moving between the rows of plants. His mind had been a jumble of concerns during the tour that he hadn't noticed a section of the interior was blocked off with thick sheets of plastic. Ginger lifted the edge of one and ducked in and held it so Harold could follow.

Inside was like a sauna, reminding him of how he'd felt in the Middle World. The space wasn't overly large, just big enough for two benches butted up against the adjoining walls, and another table placed in the middle. Ginger laid the muslin cloth next to the cotton balls, now a dirty brown with his dried blood, and the blue handkerchief which held his sweat. Next to those items were three average sized pots, a bag of soil and three spindly looking plants with their roots wrapped in damp paper towels.

"These plants are what you could call family heirlooms, brought over with my family from the Old World. They're potent when grown to maturity, dried and then used in any type of green tea. You drink the tea twice a day for three months, if it's going to be able to help you, you should begin to see results by then. What makes the process so," she looked up at him and smiled, "impossible is the experience you've just been through."

Harold watched as Ginger began to cut up the cotton balls, handkerchief and muslin into tiny pieces. As she worked those pieces into the soil, she continued to explain. "My family was gifted with a unique ability. Some might consider it an earth magic. But you can see why I'd hesitate to use that term with you before experiencing the three Worlds."

Harold listened to her now plausible explanation.

Her fingers dug into the soil, turning it over and over and over. "Somewhere along the line we married into a family with the gift to harness the energies within our human emotions, made even more potent when shed through various fluids, such as blood, sweat or tears.

The story is that my great-great-great-great grandmother was the first to understand this unique combination, and as with most new things, it frightened those around her. Not just those unable to see magic, but those who could. It threatened the established way of things. So she fled to the New World, full of promise."

Ginger unwrapped each paper towel from the plants' roots and placed them in the soil. "She taught her daughter, who taught her daughter and well, you get the idea."

As her fingers pressed the soil in around the plant, it didn't surprise Harold to see the end of her fingertips glow with an unearthly green. She glanced over at him. "I'm merely activating the ingredients you provided. The roots will absorb them and bind the plant and its properties to your body. This medicine is only for you."

She wiped her hands off on her pants and turned to face him. "Standard disclaimer, there's no guarantee this will work. It should help reduce the cancer, or at least pause it from spreading. But everything has its own way of being, of working out according to the laws that govern us. Do you think you understand?"

"I...I believe so."

"That's the key. It'll be hard once you leave, but you need to keep believing in the impossible. When these are ready to be shipped, I'll call you. I ship priority, so they should get to you two days after we talk."

Harold intently listened as Ginger once again went over the nondisclosure agreements, working to impress upon him how important it was he not to tell anyone what he'd seen, not just on her farm but in the other Worlds. Those experiences were for him alone.

Her words echoed through his thoughts as he thanked her several times before getting back into his rental car and beginning the trip to his hotel. For the first time since they had given him the diagnosis, Harold felt at peace. He knew there would still be days of sorrow, of frustration, but his anger was gone. Life was finite and yet infinite. Each day was a gift, one he'd cherish and where he'd strive to create fresh memories not only for himself but for his family.

The medicine may not cure my cancer, he thought, but this experience cured something else, buried inside of me I hadn't realized had been festering. He thought back to some conversations he'd had with Sharon, or the prompts she'd given during their group sessions. She'd focused on each one of them, of the pain, guilt, remorse and sorrow which had settled inside of each person like a fungus. A nasty growth which had blotted out the good memories and the joy in sharing another day with the ones they loved.

Harold glanced down at the picture of his family, reached out and ran his fingers along its edges. He couldn't wait to get back home.

Heidi Moone remembers the gardens of her childhood which were patches of workable ground alongside the roads of Newfoundland. She remembers racing the frost—working into the night, running through the garden plot, pulling up potatoes as fast as her child-sized hands could manage. Icy breath hanging in the air. Bonfires crackling along the garden's edge. A desperate attempt to beat the cold before it destroyed the food her family needed to survive the winter.

In time, that land would become a cemetery where the occasional potato turned up when the graves were dug for the new "residents". This mental image may have stuck in her subconscious and informed her darkly delightful story.

A Most Unusual Garden

GREY THUMB

Heidi Moone

MIRABELLE LOCKLEY WAS THE PERFECT cousin to spend a vacation with, especially an unexpected vacation, which was what Jasper Knucker was experiencing at the moment.

He wasn't entirely sure his little sister, Madeleine, felt the same way, but then, nine-year-old Madeleine, 'do not call me Maddy', was more engrossed with complicated books and strange, delicate mechanisms than she was with interacting with other children. As she was five years his junior, Jasper often felt there was an unfathomable gulf between them as siblings.

Their older sister, Cordelia, was a magnificent alien creature all her own, obsessed with gowns, invitations, balls, and things that were over Jasper's head entirely. At eighteen, four years older than him, her world had become something that decidedly excluded younger siblings.

A Most Unusual Garden

And what of robust, chubby baby brother Earnest? He rarely left his nanny's side, not having taken on a disposition yet, apart from endlessly cheerful and prone to napping. At the age of four, Jasper expected a bit more from him — Madeleine, at four, had been making toys in the nursery explode with the judicious use of rock sugar candies and other ingredients — but overall, perhaps it was a blessing for their mother that she had one child who wasn't inclined to the dramatic at all?

Not that Jasper counted himself as dramatic. Leave that for Cordelia, whose social skills were as close to flawless as someone not counted in the angelic hosts could accomplish, or Madeleine, who possibly might take over the world, or at least a good portion of the British Empire.

In light of all that, Mirabelle was like a balm on the soul. She had been properly raised, though not so proper as to be insufferable (sorry, Cordelia). She was possessed of an innate sense of humor, especially inadvertent humor, like the maids one day mistaking what needed to be packed versus unpacked for an impending vacation, resulting in a lot of confusion and then something of a squabble until the truth came to light.

And Mirabelle was prone to just enough adventure, if you asked Jasper. She liked going out of the sedate gardens her father was quite proud of, and prowling through the hills to find new places to see, just for the sake of seeing them.

This was, perhaps, the quality Jasper appreciated the most. And since they were both fourteen, this would possibly be the last summer he could accompany her. At any moment, someone in their family would notice that Mirabelle was 'quite a young lady' and then she'd be saddled with a chaperone for any and all activities.

And said activities certainly wouldn't involve an afternoon prowl outside one's father's country estate.

Jasper wasn't quite sure why young ladies got chaperones and young men did not, but he was reasonably convinced it was unfair. How did one get on with girls once they started to transform into women?

Of course, seeing some of the stuffed and dressed young men who called on his older sister didn't leave him with a lot of comfort over the future. The future for 'quite a young gentleman' seemed to involve clothing one couldn't run around in at all, and endless small talk about things that didn't seem either interesting or important.

"You are entirely too lost in thought, Jas," Mirabelle, at just that moment, interrupted his mental ponderings. He did have a tendency, his mother had cautioned him, to overthink things on occasion.

Men should be filled with action, apparently, but at least Jasper was spared that concern, being still a young boy.

"I was just thinking about my sisters," he explained. "You're very different from them."

"I suppose it may be difficult to have a few years between you all," Mirabelle nodded as she finished putting on her patent leather boots with her button hook flashing in the morning sun as she pulled the black pearl buttons through their holes. "Being an only child, I can only pity you so much, you realize."

Jasper nodded. Mirabelle's parents did dote on her, as they adored children — they had even offered to take on Madeleine at one point — but for some reason he couldn't fathom, they simply hadn't had more than the one.

Of course, the realm of having children was still a taboo topic. Stork stories and cabbage patches aside, Jasper was now perfectly aware that it had something to do with his mother's occasional rounded belly. Earnest was the most recent proof of this. Beyond that, and it needing to be a mother-and-father situation, ignorance, Jasper had decided, was clearly bliss.

Mirabelle put on her sun bonnet, and tied it with ease. Jasper had his hat, which meant neither of them would be too sunburned if they opted for the route of a nice morning in the garden, versus an exploration further afield.

"Well, Earnest has hardly become an actual person yet, so if your parents are keen to try him out, I would recommend it heartily," Jasper offered as they headed toward the back garden.

"So thoughtful, giving up your only brother to ease our familial plight," Mirabelle smiled, all the way from her generous mouth to her lively grey-green eyes.

She had the family eyes, the same as his mother's and aunt's in coloration. For Jasper's part, he was reduced to what his mother charitably called a cheerful brown, or as his father stated it, mud-colored.

"Couldn't even get to green, like your cousin, let alone blue," the elder Argus Knucker had said, once or twice. Of course, Mr. Knucker, of Knucker, Peabody, and Graves, had cold blue eyes like the ocean on a sunless day.

None of Argus' children had blue eyes, or anything approaching it. Madeleine's were so dark as to seem to be black, while Cordelia's eyes were so light they almost seemed golden in the right light. Even pudgy Earnest had pudgy chocolate brown eyes.

"Anything I can do for family," Jasper nodded agreeably.

Out in the garden, they could start off with a bit of a ramble, although Jasper was eager to see what Mirabelle might have in her sturdy wicker basket, covered in a red and white checked cloth, as was proper. He did poke at it dutifully, only to have his hand and his verbal inquiry both swatted away.

"The basket has all the things a young lady might need for a morning excursion," she said as she waved at the gardener, who was seeing to some topiary.

The gardener bobbed his head, but notably did not wave back.

Jasper finally learned that underneath her checkered cloth there were snacks, two sodas in bottles, a slingshot—wherever had she gotten such a thing—and a couple of well-worn books.

"We may not be missed at lunch, if we go where our noses lead us," she explained. "Mother and Aunt Winnie are planning to be at the Temperance Hall today for a luncheon, and your sister's going to be at a friend's house."

Jasper nodded. Cordelia had already left this morning, in a proper carriage, to visit with female friends and, no doubt, talk about young men and suitable marriages.

"Do you want to follow the river upstream?"

Jasper looked at Mirabelle, and grinned.

"I thought you'd never ask," he said, finding the world as agreeable a place as it could possibly be.

ON A PREVIOUS EXCURSION, THREE days before, they had started to follow the river, really more of a stream with pretentions, toward its origins.

However, a delightful abandoned orchard had beckoned them, and within a good half-hour's walk, they were faced with the same conundrum.

"I would adore owning this orchard," Mirabelle decided as she sat in a rather sturdy swing hanging from what had to be the Monarch of all apple trees. Jasper sat on a bench that needed attention more than the swing, but was suited for the purpose of sitting, nonetheless.

They both ate apples, but not from the orchard, as its apples were not yet ripe. Basket apples, Jasper thought with amusement.

"You would go into the apple business," Jasper nodded. "It's how I've always seen you, Mirabelle."

She snorted in an unladylike way.

"I probably would have to, owning an orchard," she mused. "But I would tidy it up, don't you think? Look how those arrogant weeds are starting to crowd in, and choke things out. Look how unruly the saplings are. No respect for their elders, as mother would say."

Now, Jasper rather liked the charm of an orchard not ruthlessly minded within an inch of its life, but he opted not to speak about that. Neither of them owned the orchard, or would ever own the orchard, so what matter its upkeep?

"So, we can read here, like we did on Tuesday, or we can venture on," he said, getting up, dusting off his pants a little with some random slaps of his hands, and walking over to where an intriguing sort of stick had been left against a tree, looking for all the world like a walking stick a shepherd might use.

"I do so love a swing. You know, father simply won't install one in our garden," Mirabelle swung, higher and higher, her play dress and petticoats billowing out in one direction and then closing around her legs in the other. "When I have my own house and garden, a swing there will be."

If her husband allowed it. But Jasper didn't say anything to that. If Mirabelle's husband didn't allow her a swing, he would, he decided out of the blue, put a magnificent swing in his own garden in the back of the house he'd have. Someday.

Although, thinking about it, that was quite a long way off.

Then Mirabelle leapt, at the pinnacle of her forward motion, and flew through the air quite brilliantly, a cry of joy torn from her in that moment as her limbs all seemed inclined to fly off in different directions from the forward motion of her body overall.

Despite all that, she quite landed on her feet, although Jasper had feared for her neck, and only her left glove's fingertips got stained from where she reached out to steady herself.

"Oh, so marvelous!" Her cheeks were red with excitement and her eyes danced with mischief. "Let's go and see what's up the river, Jas."

He bowed, and waved his walking staff at her. Undaunted, Mirabelle hunted around until she was able to find a branch more suited for a lady's walking stick. It even had a knobby end to serve as a proper handle for her and, basket in her other hand, off they went.

"It's simply lovely to have you all visit, you know, mother's much more anxious about me wandering off to have an adventure when we don't have company," Mirabelle noted after several minutes.

"Well, we weren't expecting a visit, but I'm just as happy. Madeleine is all fretful, not having access to her secret laboratory, but I suspect she'll make do," Jasper mused, and Mirabelle grinned.

"I may, or may not, have settled her away in the attic," she admitted.

"Hopefully the attic's not overly flammable," Jasper said after a moment.

Mirabelle's laughter was entirely not comforting.

A few minutes later, they crested a small hill and found a sort of crossroads before them. Jasper grinned. Now this, this was promising.

"Oh, heavenly, this trail intersects with another," Mirabelle was flush, with rosy cheeks and dancing eyes. "Three opportunities for adventure, so we can return, time and time again, and see what's down every pathway."

They scampered down the hill, Jasper already considering their options from the footpath.

The choices seemed rather intriguing. Their footpath intersected with a wider, cobbled way that led from a black house eclipsed by trees to what could only be described as a quaint little bridge, wide enough across for perhaps three people walking, or one person on horseback, that crossed the brook and then ended in mist.

"How odd," Mirabelle mused. "It's not foggy on this side at all, Jas."

"Remember, when we were eight, how it rained on one side of the road when we were at the beach, and not on the other side?"

They grinned at one another. That had been a delightful day, filled with sandcastles and ice cream, and an episode where one of the children on the beach had picked up an overturned bucket to find three-year-old Madeleine had contrived to pile up hermit crabs within it, who then ran amok.

"That was as peculiar as this," Mirabelle decided.

If they continued straight through on their footpath, there was an intriguing twist in the brook, and in the distance, Jasper thought he could hear the shrill laughter of children over another hill, and some splashing noises.

"Do you want to meet up with children in your neighborhood?" Jasper asked Mirabelle, who frowned and looked thoughtfully toward the sounds.

"You know," she said, in a quiet tone, "There are actually no children in the vicinity of the house, and there haven't been since several members of a family died in a boating accident on a nearby pond, about twenty years ago."

Jasper listened to the distant trails of laughter, and swallowed.

"I'm kidding, you idiot," Mirabelle sputtered with laughter as she swatted at his shoulder. "Oh, your face, Jasper, I simply can't!"

She leaned on one of the bridge posts and laughed, swiping her eyes for tears as her cheeks became ruddy. Jasper pressed his lips together, none too impressed at having been exposed as both gullible and cowardly in one fell stroke.

"Well, you're a complete arse," he declared, and she gasped, her eyes wide with astonishment.

"You sailor, look at the mouth on you!" She shook her head, still smiling broadly. "I think that's the Headley children, Jas, honestly, their oldest boy does nothing but pull hair, and he's a solid year older than both of us."

"Well, that leaves us with a spooky house, or the bridge and the fog," Jasper decided. But Mirabelle was already on the bridge, her walking stick making a solid thunk sound as she set out.

"Hair pulling," she tossed behind her, and Jasper admitted, those sorts of boys were not the ideal sort to pal around with anyway.

Their boots clattered on the bridge, and Jasper felt a chill at the midway point. Glancing back, it seemed to him the bridge looked longer than it logically was.

But then Jasper's boots struck soil, and he almost ran into Mirabelle, who stood there, leaning on her makeshift cane like a little old lady.

"It's the wrong time of the summer to have just turned your garden," she said, contemplatively.

It was true. Jasper surveyed the path leading away from the bridge, laid out in neat, bone-white stones about the width of his thumb. It was wide enough for three people to walk side-by-side, like the bridge, but it meandered back and forth in a lazy sort of spiral between fields that had been turned sometime recently, as nothing was growing just yet.

"I wonder what they planted?"

His voice was somewhat foreign to his ears. It was the hush, for no birds sang on this side of the river, and they could no longer hear the splashing and play of the children through the fog that curled to envelop them.

"Hardly a garden, I would think. And it doesn't look like root vegetables or anything like that, no neat and tidy rows. It is spacious, though," Mirabelle said as she began trotting along the path. Jasper took a deep breath and then followed his cousin, who of course needed an escort. "I must say, the path is terribly winding, don't you think?"

It was, twisting and bending according to no rule Jasper could discern. They walked here, and there, and still hadn't moved particularly far from the bridge at all.

"Toss it, I'm going rogue," she said at last, lifting her skirts to head over the earth.

"Mirabelle, I don't think it's wise. Don't you...smell something off? I think there's fertilizer down," Jasper frowned, and Mirabelle's forward motion came to an immediate halt.

"Mother will be ever-so cross if I turn up with anything like that on my dress, even if it is a play dress," Mirabelle nodded, sniffling the air. "Ugh, such a stench, isn't it?"

Jasper silently agreed, as he crouched down, hands on his walking staff, to get a closer look at a sprout that seemed to be on the cusp of breaking through the soil.

The smell was really something, and his eyes watered a little as he squinted. Something about it was so familiar, but his mind couldn't quite place it.

"Jasper," Mirabelle's voice had taken on an unexpected hush, and Jasper leaned in a little, tilting his head to one side. "Jasper."

At the very moment Jasper's brain clicked the pieces together, and told him that was no sprout, it was a finger with a curving nail, he felt a hand grab his collar and drag him backward.

"Jasper!" Mirabelle hissed, and he turned to see a full, human hand slowly pushing up through the soil on the other side of the path.

"Ahhh," he gasped, not quite able to draw enough air into his lungs to scream as he might like.

The hand was not a normal hand in any respect. It had the correct number of fingers, but they were a sick, waxy sort of grey, and they twitched rather than move as a regular person's hand might, to pick something up, or point something out.

This hand spasmed. Then it inched higher, a wrist beginning to emerge from the soil with excruciating slowness.

A Most Unusual Garden

Off to the left, a second hand had appeared. And behind it, more hands were peeking forth.

Jasper, with difficulty, glanced back at the finger he'd been so absorbed with, to find it, too, was now fully a hand, and it was spread out, as though waiting for someone to take it and pull.

In that moment, Mirabelle's own hand parodied it as she reached out to Jasper, firmly took hold of his right hand, and began to run.

With her skirts bunched in her other hand, she pulled him, not back toward the bridge, but further into the estate.

"What are you doing?" Jasper felt he didn't quite shriek it at her, as he saw one hand, of the dozens blossoming around them like a mockery of spring lilies, had fully emerged, and a small mound had formed where...no. No, there were hands. There couldn't be heads.

"There is a road," she said. "We just have to reach the road, Jas, and it'll be okay."

He wanted to pick her up and run back to the bridge. Jasper was rationally sure he couldn't pick her up and run back to the bridge.

"The bridge," he gasped, gesturing behind them, though Mirabelle wouldn't see it.

"It's too late for that," she said, her hand tightening, grown clammy with fear.

It would be both their lives if he listened to his cousin. The bridge wasn't that far away, and they could find people, they could go across the water. It was safe, back there. Everything had been normal, before crossing the bridge.

An elbow broke through the turned earth, like an unruly creeper vine.

And resplendent, on the other side, the first head started to emerge, turned toward them, as a flower's face would seek out the sun.

The eyes, black and oily, followed their frantic passage, but slowly, as though too viscous to make the effort easy.

"No, no," Jasper said, feeling the apple in his stomach churn and threaten to reappear violently. He picked up the pace then, half picked-up Mirabelle, and began to run ahead of her. All around them, little hands were beginning to appear, and the earth was buckling with the promise of more, and more.

"Jasper, don't cross the path," Mirabelle said, and pulled him up short.

He'd, in fact, been about to bolt over a part of the path, rather than take an abominable curlicue to reach a place not particularly far away in front of them.

"Mirabelle, something impossible and grotesque surrounds us!"

"It's a zombie garden, Jasper, I didn't realize it until it was too late," Mirabelle said, as they rounded a corner and ended up with three path choices ahead of them, like a maze. "Abominable to have come across it, but we must be quick to escape it at all."

"Zombie? I've never heard of such a word," Jasper gaped at his cousin, and this strange, fearful knowledge she seemed to be in possession of. "Please tell me this is...a mad prank you're pulling on me, with some friends of yours."

They both stared down at a beautiful, emaciated face. Blonde hair was still coming out of the soil, and so Jasper presumed it was a female...zombie. Her eyes remained closed as her hands fluttered restlessly, twitching as they tried to decide if they would push, try to grasp something that simply wasn't there, or just remain, like white-grey lilies.

"I'm going to be sick," Jasper breathed.

"Don't you dare," Mirabelle sounded indignant, more than horrified, as she grabbed him and fairly dragged him off to the path on the right. "There's a road, Jas, we're almost there."

"I don't think these things will be much challenged by a road," Jasper said feebly. "What's a zombie?"

"It's a person who's been reanimated after death or great tribulation," Mirabelle said, using her stick to gingerly poke away a flopping hand that was almost over the pebble barrier. "That's not a good sign at all."

"What could possibly make this worse?" Jasper said, and then a moment later was presented with quite an answer.

He managed to dash ahead of his cousin once more and recommence dragging her, as they reached a section of the odious garden that seemed to have been planted, for lack of a better descriptor, with children. Their chubby little arms had not become wasted in death as some of the adults had been, but were plump and grotesque as they wriggled out of the garden earth more like grubs than plants.

"Be careful," Mirabelle gasped. But Jasper knew the rules, didn't he? It was like hop-score, after all. Stay within the lines or you'd lose your turn.

People, zombies, were creeping, creeping, some of them past their chests, a few of them down to their waists. They had been dressed well for this haunting moment, colorfully, even. He saw pearls around one woman's neck, and yellow satin gloves stained with dirt were on a young girl not much older than his sister, Cordelia. Her now-dull hair was done in ringlets that bounced as she shuddered, emerging from the soil.

Jasper swallowed a sudden lump in his throat warring with sick, as he stumbled a little, coming on the dust and pounded flatness of a road. He half-fell and staggered in a wide circle, his knees aching as they kept him on his feet. "Oh," he gasped, as Mirabelle helped him stay upright.

"I think we've done it," she said, but then they turned to see, on the other side of the road, that the garden in fact continued. Mirabelle's face fell, and she looked so surprised it might've been comedic if Jasper hadn't wanted this all to be over so badly.

"But zombie gardens should be confined by the works of men and the boundaries of nature," she said, shaking her head. "Unless someone has planted two of them? But why?"

As Jasper opened his mouth to ask what on earth his cousin could possibly mean by all this, a zombie unexpectedly pulled herself out of the earth by one leg, and made a raucous clacking noise with her jaw.

Making a bit of a high-pitched whine, Jasper was surprised to hear the sound of horses in the distance, and he looked up to see a most welcome sight coming up the road toward them.

"Here, here!" He started to wave his arms, dropping his walking staff in his haste. The staff fell across the little line of pebbles, but it didn't matter, there would be a rescue.

The carriage was all in black, which was not unusual, and the horses were black to match, all four of them, their heads tossing with as they raced toward the two children on the road.

A Most Unusual Garden

"Jasper, we must run," Mirabelle's voice was low and firm. "Stop flapping your arms about."

"But it's a carriage," Jasper turned to stare at his cousin, and felt scared.

Mirabelle looked...enraged, she looked like a stranger, her face was so drawn and pale. She looked older than her fourteen years.

"That will not be a rescuer," she predicted, her voice almost choking the words out, and then she gasped as a figure lunged at her over the break in the pebbled barrier caused by the fall of Jasper's walking staff.

Mirabelle beat the male zombie, wearing a top hat in a style from perhaps three or four years ago, with her makeshift walking stick, her lips pulled back as she took her stick in hand and swung it like a cricket mallet, dislocating the zombie's jaw.

Jasper just shook his head, looking around him. On the opposite side of the road fingers were starting to poke through the soil as well, and he had every expectation that, in short order, things would be as dismal on one side of the road as the other.

At that moment, he was almost trampled to death by the horses.

"Mirabelle Eiderdown, it is time."

This wasn't the man driving the carriage who spoke. That man, garbed in black, and actually wearing a mask like some sort of criminal, stared straight ahead, as though nothing horrific was taking place.

Jasper stumbled around the horses—one snapped at him—and found his cousin was staring at a man who was dressed, astonishingly, in a uniformly pale grey color, with a top hat and respectability oozing from his pores.

"It is certainly not time, as I am only fourteen years old," she said stiffly.

"And her name is Mirabelle Lockley, sir, I am her cousin," Jasper interjected. "She is my cousin, and in my company."

"So proper," the man said, his accent quite upper-crust, though his sneer was quite schoolyard, if you asked Jasper. "Mirabelle, the contract was clear that you had until your eighteenth birthday, or the termination of your natural life, which is imminent, let me assure you."

"Did your master plant this zombie garden?" Mirabelle demanded, while Jasper gingerly picked up his staff and started to prod two zombies with it. They weren't particularly inclined to come near the carriage, at least.

"It is of little consequence now," the man said. "You will accompany me, or you will be in breach of the contract that was agreed to."

"Excuse me, but no one's life is actually being terminated," Jasper said. "We can simply get a ride with you, sir, and alert the authorities to, uh, all of this to-do and have them straighten this out."

"What sort of cousin might he be, to be so ignorant?" The man raised an eyebrow at Jasper, who was peeved both because raising a single eyebrow was a desirable skill that Jasper lacked, and because he didn't feel he was acutely ignorant, and suddenly acutely felt it, at the exact same time.

"His mother is an Eiderdown as well, but of course, he is a boy," Mirabelle said with alacrity. "He is of no consequence to your master."

"Perhaps that is a decision the master would make, rather than a foolish girl who wanders through a zombie garden," the man declared, his lips twitching, as though he wanted to smile cruelly, but didn't quite have the experience in smiling to accomplish it.

Mirabelle, her sunbonnet missing, her nose smudged, and her basket partially emptied by their mad dash, did not look confident as she stared at Jasper.

"My cousin must be removed from danger as well, and then I will go with you as per the contract," she declared.

"Mirabelle, no, I forbid you to go with this strange and off-putting rogue," Jasper shook his head. Turning back, he could see the garden in its full 'bloom' now, with women's dresses billowing out and men in brightly colored suits weaving back and forth, almost completely out of the ground.

"She does not have a choice."

"There's always a choice," Jasper said, repeating words his father had often said when discussing matters with colleagues from work after dinner.

In that moment, the man stepped out of the carriage, walked over to Mirabelle, and grabbed her by the arm.

"No, there is not," he said, throwing her bodily toward the carriage. Mirabelle had dropped the basket, and Jasper swept it up at once.

"If you think you're going to hit me with that, you little snot, I will personally bury you up to your bloody neck in that garden with your new friends."

Jasper swallowed. The man was actually tall, taller than Jasper's father, for a certainty, and had that 'I am violent' air about him that Jasper had hitherto only experienced in the schoolyard.

"Jas, run, you need to run," Mirabelle said, and there were tears in her voice. "They will be afraid of the carriage, and perhaps that will be enough if you run after it."

"No," Jasper said, setting his jaw. He picked up one of the bone white stones from the now-scuffled path, and he fitted it in the slingshot that Mirabelle had stuffed into the bottom of the basket.

When they'd been younger, he and Mirabelle had been quite keen to become expert slingshot people, as they'd been forbidden the noble practice of archery. Now, he took aim at the flank of the horse nearest him.

With a silent apology, Jasper hit the horse in the rear and it bolted, causing its equally high-strung cohort to go with it. The coachman, who'd been so meticulously stiff and studiously ignorant of events, almost fell off, and certainly didn't have any particular control as the carriage suddenly vanished down the road.

"You little shit," the man said, his accent suddenly not as upper-crust as before. His eyes were murderous as he turned on Jasper.

"My cousin said no," Jasper said, all the panic leaving him, strangely, as the zombies began to weave their way past him, their hands reaching, not for Jasper, but for the stranger who'd tried to hurt Mirabelle.

"Jasper!"

It wasn't Mirabelle who shrieked, but an unexpected voice. The voice of the angel of their family, Cordelia.

What on earth could his sister be doing here?

She was, as he turned to look, in a one-horse buggy she was driving, but Cordelia wasn't alone. His sister, Madeleine, was already out and running toward them with some sort of device strapped to her back.

"I am sadly used to being right, but this one time, honestly, I could've borne the ridicule of being in error," his little sister snapped as Jasper was fairly in the throng of the bodies of the dead, surging in a mass onto the road.

But strangely, none of them laid a finger on him at all.

Mirabelle was quite audible, and Jasper could hear the man swearing as his baby sister swung what looked like a hose back and forth, though nothing more than a light mist seemed to come from it.

"Back, back, you cretins! I know some of you have ears!"

The zombies did begin to go back off the road. Jasper was completely confounded.

One zombie girl, about the same age as he and Mirabelle, stopped a moment and looked at him sadly with her swirling black eyes. She wore a sunbonnet and a pretty flower print dress, and Jasper put his hand out for her before a living hand reached around her to pull him away from all of the death.

"I believe this should put your employer at rest," Cordelia said, descending from the buggy as Madeleine hissed through clenched teeth at the now-retreating zombies, who seemed much diminished by the curious mist she'd been spraying, a mist that now put Jasper strangely in mind of the mist that had hung over the land prior to their arrival. "There is no contract broken if Mirabelle is not in mortal danger, after all."

"What is he?" The man was staring at Jasper now. "They should have consumed him."

"I guess you don't know how to make proper zombies after all," Madeleine scoffed.

"Manners," Cordelia said with a tut-tut. "Mr. Cottonmouth, is it not? You have no place here, you see. You are the one in breach of contract, I believe. You have laid a hand on my cousin. A sternly written letter will result."

Mr. Cottonmouth, if that was, indeed, his name, said a word that had Jasper scrambling to cover his little sister's ears, while Madeleine simply laughed in astonishment, once. "Ha!"

By now, the black carriage had turned around, and the no-longer-oblivious coachman stood up.

"I am leaving, Mr. Cottonmouth," he said.

Without another word, the man in the grey suit stalked to the carriage, got in, and they promptly thundered past. Before they went too far down the road the carriage, for lack of a better descriptor, vanished, just before they were to go around a bend in the road.

"Clearly, I've hit my head and gone mad," Jasper muttered, looking back at the zombie garden.

The zombies had returned to their jumbled beds and rows, but they waited now, watching the little tableau on the road, or something akin to watching, with their oily black eyes.

"I have no clue how to put them all back," he heard Madeleine said, and she sounded fretful. "This is quite shocking."

"How did you know?" Mirabelle, gasping, had run into Cordelia's outstretched arms. "It was so horrid, mother will be so cross with me for not recognizing that this was a zombie garden, freshly turned!"

"Our own mother had a Notion in the middle of her outing, and I was able to make it back in time," Cordelia explained. "No harm done, Mirabelle, you were quite brave."

"Do you all know about this, this…" Jasper shook his head, not even having words for it all. "What is happening?"

"It's all over now, except for the garden," Madeleine explained. "We can have tea and you'll be much better for it, I should say."

"You're nine, and you know, what? What is all this?"

"It's never been a problem you needed to concern yourself with, sweet boy, this is a problem strictly for the women in our family," Cordelia said, lifting her spotless skirts and gesturing. Jasper didn't go to her, not even a step. "Our maternal line is called the Eiderdown, and we have great responsibilities, Jasper, but they needn't be a burden for you."

"Perhaps we can just blow them to smithereens," Madeleine mused, off to one side.

"Can't we just leave them for the time being? The person who arranged for the garden is certainly responsible for it," Mirabelle said.

"No, we can't be the sort of people who see a problem and don't take action. That's not the Eiderdown way," Cordelia explained.

Jasper tilted his head, looking at them all. The Eiderdown women, with their secret name and their secret lives. Even his older sister, who seemed as ordinary as she was wonderful, clearly had some edge of uncanniness to her.

"You don't have to stand for it, you know," a voice murmured.

Jasper startled and looked.

Amidst the colorful zombies, a man in white stood, stock still while the creatures undulated, almost with the breeze.

He was a remarkably ordinary man. Not too tall, nor too short. His suit was good, but not startling. His eyes did not seem to hold any innate cruelty in them. Rather, he seemed sympathetic.

"I, too, came from similar circumstances," he explained. "Dreadful thing. Women with no small measure of power, but power can blind you to things, Jasper. It is Jasper, isn't it?"

"It is, sir, if it please you, Jasper Knucker."

"Ah, you would go far in the world if you laid claim to the Eiderdown name, you know, but I respect a young man who stands on his own two feet."

"Might this be your garden, sir?"

"Why yes, it happens to be my garden," the man admitted. "And forgive my manners, dreadful of me. Master Knucker, I am Mr. Graves, of course."

"You make light of the situation, I am sure," Jasper said, gaping a little as he looked around at a garden of graves, if you went to the heart of it.

He stepped into the garden proper, as the man had turned and begun to walk away. To Jasper it didn't seem particularly unnatural to do so. His fear of the dead had drained away, and they were sad now, with touches of strange beauty to them.

"Not at all, it is my own family name," Mr. Graves explained. "I am, in fact, a distant relation to your father's partner in business. I was ever-so surprised to have this outcome arise. I am not the person Miss Eiderdown is contracted to marry on her eighteenth birthday, and so I wished to offer my apologies for this misunderstanding when I happened to notice your plight."

"Being attacked by these sorts?" Jasper had found the sad girl again with the sun bonnet and the patterned dress, she drew his eye.

"They wouldn't attack you, Jasper, though I appreciate how startling they can be in the first moments, and of course the smell. No, indeed, I think you may have, as we would say, Potential."

"Jasper, dear goodness, Jasper!"

Cordelia's voice was quite distant, and Jasper turned back to see himself surrounded by a riot of color, all stained with dark, rich earth.

"You certainly can return to your loving sisters and your family, with their deceptions and lies. And the next time something untoward happens, why, you may end up in a sticky wicket, don't you think?"

"I just want to know what's going on," Jasper noted. "And I want to be,

I guess, helpful in some way." He thought of the moment that terrible man had grabbed Mirabelle and thrown her about. "People should be decent to one another, sir."

"It would be presumptuous of me to ask you to make decisions on the heels of such an ordeal, and you should wait and see what your family has to say about the circumstances. But, should you decide that they are lacking in their sincerity, please do consider my apology for the day, and feel free to contact me to discuss opportunities for the future. I see greatness in you, Jasper."

And Mr. Graves handed Jasper a crisp white card with gold lettering that declared Mr. Z. Graves to be a consultant. Jasper knew the office address was in a notable part of London.

"Now, I shall remove the gardens in their entirety."

"Uh, are these people really, you know, dead?" Jasper looked at some of the younger lot, bumbling about, and his heart went out to them. Death was never kind, but seemed particularly cruel when it came to children.

"Death is a nuanced topic," Mr. Graves said, sounding thoughtful. "Nevertheless, these people are not, in this moment, in a living condition as you yourself are."

And he led Jasper to a small, empty section of the garden, swept his hand, and little white pebbles fell in a neat circle around the confused boy. Then Graves took out, of all things, a little tin pipe and proceeded to play a small tune on it.

The pipe was not particularly shrill, and yet the sound managed to echo. Slowly, and then quickly, the ground churned and people sank and shuddered back into it. The girl in the patterned dress was one of the last to go, and behind her, Jasper could see his alarmed family members frantically gesturing at him.

Where had Mr. Graves gone?

He'd vanished, in between one note and the next.

Of course, Jasper had the man's card. But he pocketed the thing before Madeleine, the bravest, thundered into the now mercilessly churned field to come and grab him, looking quite beside herself.

"Did you do that, Jasper?" She was solemn as she asked it.

"I don't know what's going on," Jasper declared.

"They didn't lay a finger on him," he thought he heard Mirabelle say to Cordelia as they returned to the road. And that was true, Jasper reflected, nothing at all had actually happened to him physically, beyond being in the grip of utter terror.

"I do require an explanation," he said, trying, and failing, to raise a single eyebrow, though his voice didn't quaver even a little, a victory for the morning, he thought as he realized the sun was still not even at its zenith for the day.

Cordelia looked at him for a long moment, eye to eye, before coming to carefully gather him up — she wore a cream-colored dress that was mercifully free of stain or blemish.

"Jasper, sometimes there are strange things in the world, but most of the time, there aren't any at all," she murmured. "Mummy can explain some of this to you, I'm sure, but if you accept that this was an aberrant episode, you don't need to dwell on it, and can have a rather lovely life, if you'd prefer."

"Oh, just tell him, coddling him will just make him angry, or sulky, which is probably worse," Madeleine predicted, and Jasper threw her a look that was half-irritation, and half-gratitude.

"Jasper, do please, I beseech you to let it go," Mirabelle asked him then, coming up and smiling at him, a smile that no longer reached all the way to her red-rimmed eyes. "For the love of me, please, it's so pleasant to spend days with you and never have the trouble of all this."

"That man almost stole you away," Jasper began, but then threw his hands in the air. "All right, all right, for now, but how shall we get back? There's barely enough room in the buggy for you, Cordelia, though you made it here with Madeleine, somehow."

At that moment, a clatter announced the arrival of Mirabelle's family carriage, complete with their ruddy-faced coachman.

"Your mother's quite keen to have a word with you, Miss Lockley," he said, and suddenly, all supernatural topics of conversation seemed to have vanished as thoroughly as the zombies had.

As they pulled into the estate home, Madeleine reached across and patted Jasper on the knee.

"Personally, Jasper, you only have one chance to live a good, straightforward life," she said. "Ignorance is bliss."

"Clearly you know quite a bit for a girl who hasn't even turned ten yet," Jasper hissed.

"And if I could just be, well, an ordinary girl who cares about hair and getting a new dress, it might be nice to try that out," Madeleine said, looking dubious about her own pronouncement, and Jasper laughed at her.

"Not since you poisoned your nanny when you were four have you wanted to be ordinary, not for a minute."

"That was purely an accident, and I guess you just don't know me as well as you think," Madeleine said, getting out of the carriage.

As their mothers descended on them and much fuss ensued, Jasper was taken aside by his mother a minute, who looked him over rather thoroughly, staring at his face for a long moment, and then instructed him to go take a bath.

"I have called for your father to come and talk with you," she said, her eyes looking pinched as she spoke. They always looked unhappy when the topic of her husband arose, nowadays.

"The girls all asked me...not to speak about this," Jasper muttered, and his mother embraced him, just as she always had.

"I can see the pain in your eyes, Jasper, and I see more there as well," she said. "I think your father should be consulted."

And so, Jasper found himself waiting for a man who had always looked at him with disappointment, his mind playing back and forth over the events of the day.

Zombies. The man in white. The carriage. The bridge. The man in grey. Zombies.

When his father shook his shoulder, Jasper was surprised to find he'd fallen asleep on his bed, as his brain had seemingly kept on with the jumble of memories, even in his dreams.

"My word," Argus Knucker's cold eyes widened in shock. "Well, I see why I've been summoned."

"I don't understand," Jasper said, feeling miserable and inclined to cry, but he was fourteen, and his father had never tolerated the outbursts of children. He tried to square his shoulders, but then, something even more alarming than zombies happened.

His father picked him up, and hugged him, as the man had never embraced him before.

"My son," he said. "I am so proud of you. Do you have any questions for me? I know today was a frightful time. To have your mother summon me so urgently, of course it must be the case."

"Father, I don't understand anything of what happened, beyond the fact it's not...scientific," Jasper said after a moment. "The girls asked me to pretend it never happened. However, it consumes my thoughts."

"You will need tutors, I believe," his father said, almost to himself. "No expense will be spared. I will consult with specialists."

"Did I imagine it?" Jasper wondered. "Have I had a breakdown?"

That might be preferable to what he believed had happened. Now that he'd slept, it all seemed entirely fanciful. As though he'd eaten some unfortunate treat and upset his stomach.

"Jasper, the world beyond our doors is very modern, scientific, and rational, as you've been raised to appreciate," Argus said, leading his son to the dresser, which had a mirror mounted at the top of it. "However, your mother's family has long had a different role to play in the world. And uncanny sort of purpose, one might say."

And Jasper used the looking glass to see a face that was at once his, and yet entirely foreign.

His eyes were now blue-grey, the same as his mother's. Which was simply impossible.

"When you see the world through different eyes, my son, anything is possible," Argus Knucker explained. "I can imagine your mother's shock, and of course your sisters and cousin. We will find the answers you need, but I would very much...appreciate it if you chose to embrace the uncanny."

"Can my eyes become normal again?" Jasper asked, confused anew by his father's unexpected, not quite warmth, but enthusiasm toward him.

"I don't know," Argus mused, a little hesitant, suddenly. "It can be investigated. I will make enquiries of my peers."

"Peabody and Graves?" Jasper blurted out, and his father's glance toward him was sudden and laced with suspicion.

"They are my business partners," he said slowly. "Jasper, I have long said that my business is the realm of adults, not of curious boys."

Jasper nodded.

"I don't know of your...other peers," he said feebly, and his father smiled again, not quite a comforting smile at all, really.

"That is true," he said. "Well, your mother has no idea of how to manage this turn, which leaves you as my responsibility, young man. We will have to have suits made, and then introductions made. Yes, yes we will."

And his father went on about these vague plans a while, answering almost nothing before leaving Jasper to the evening gloom that notably contained no promise of supper at all.

Well, Jasper thought as he stared at his new eyes in the mirror, what had been done could be undone, surely? And if that was the case, perhaps it was best to leave this as a singular incident in an otherwise rather ordinary life. A not-unpleasant life, if one felt reasonable about things.

Or perhaps he might write a letter to the mysterious Mr. Graves, the one person who'd at least been apologetic, and who had answered all of his questions. As a maid knocked on his door and revealed that, in fact, supper was taking place, Jasper felt like, if his family was determined to be mysterious, certainly, he could be secretive as well.

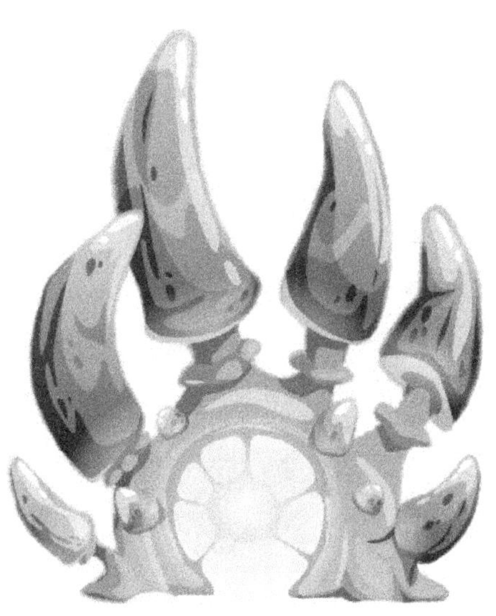

N. D. Gray grew up with a strong gardening tradition. Her family planted extensive gardens and canned or froze most of their harvests. They would pile the kitchen table high with vegetables or apples. Everyone would pitch in. Dinner would be whatever was being preserved. It required long, hard hours of work, but was worth it. No brand or person has ever surpassed her mother's canned green beans.

Her story unfolds around a different sort of family and a different sort of garden. One sown in sorrow and tended with desperate hope.

MARY, MARY

N.D. Gray

MARY STOOD IN HER GARDEN and watched the sun rise over the hills. The new light touched the shallow valley before her like pale golden water. It bled onto the scene in an otherworldly beauty and contrasted with the blue-gray line of gentle slopes to the east. Those blue-gray hills protected the Homestead where she and her companions spun out the threads of their days.

Before and below her, at the base of the short, grassy plateau on which the Homestead's buildings were built, fields of grain rippled in the morning breeze. The golden patches stretched down to the wide stream where elms and willows grew.

A flock of birds lifted from the stream-side trees. Their murmuration was a poetic harmony through the gold-washed morning, and Mary was pleased she was the sort which could appreciate such a sight.

"Mary, Mary," Clem called from the powerbays ringed like ancient standing stones in the yard before the Big House. There was an expulsion of pressure as he disengaged from his bay, power chords dropping away and the cradle locks releasing as he came fully online.

She did not turn toward him.

"Quite contrary," was Clem's reply to her silence. He stood slowly and made the metallic hollow sound that was his laughter. Why a farm hand needed to be programed with a sense of humor, she had never figured out.

She turned her head farther away, and her left eye fell from its socket. It dangled at the end of its filament coil, splitting her field of vision, one half of which now showed the grass and her painted on shoes in jumping distorted images. Exasperation routine kicking in, she sighed and fiddled with the ocular piece, working it back into place.

"Mary, Mary," Clem said as he approached across the yard and under the spreading shade tree that shadowed the place where she stood. "How does your garden grow?"

He could see for himself.

She watched the flock of birds settle down into the distant trees.

"Blackened cells and squishy jells and broken dollies in a row." Clucking his tongue in disapproval, Clem—who looked nearly as human as she did— walked away from the garden.

The morning breeze stirred the brown curls resting against her cheek. Her mouth was open and she felt a routine trying to start somewhere deep inside her processor. The faint memory of a taste bled across her tongue. The ghost of fresh mown hay and honeyed sweetness. The flavor of sadness filling her mouth.

She watched the farmhand, his long, lanky strides. Big hands swinging at his sides. Casing made to look like the rough material clothes of the humans who worked the land day in and day out.

As he followed the path down toward the fields, the utility compartment on his right arm cycled open and his skin-soft hand whirled around to be replaced by a telescoping scythe. Beneath the golden light of dawn, he set to work, tending his crops, the blue and brown casing of his body whirring with the motion as he raised and lowered his arm.

"Don't listen to him, darlings," Mary murmured to the plantlings in her garden. "You will grow tall. You will grow big. You will grow beautiful."

The three-legged bot dog wagged his tail.

She had planted him front feet down, the dirt mounding up over this back, but she'd left his tail and his head free after opening the casing on the sides to reveal the biocells and expose them to the nutrients in the soil. He barked and she scratched him behind his ear.

A squishy jell-bear burbled in its nearby resting place. Vivid pink jell-body bright against the burnt umber ground. It was planted to its arm pits and it waved its arms distractedly. "Easy now," Mary whispered, soothing the jell-bear as the touch of sunlight awoke it.

She walked among the others. The Honk Truck with big blue and orange lights on top of its square cab. They brightened and dimmed slowly and steadily. The "Big Bad Unicorn" who could barely move his nearly life-sized head, his mechanisms having locked up long ago. A line of baby dolls in all shapes and sizes—black, brown, yellow, purple, green. One leg, or two, or four. Human arms and bot arms and tentacles and no arms. Plastic, jell, metal, or TrooSkyn. Bald, mohawked, long braids, or fur. Cracked or broken. Eyes wide staring. Their quiet chorus of, "Mama", a strange bass line to the twittering melody of a hundred different dawn birdsongs.

She spoke to each one. Sweetly. Soothingly. She sang to them her own songs. Songs of growing and of being. Of history and of hope. Occasionally her hip servo chanked in protest as she squatted down, but she ignored it as she had Clem's taunting, focusing instead on her task, making sure each plantling was tucked in securely and their moisture levels were ideal. Patting the rich soil around them and dreaming of the harvest she hoped for.

When she was satisfied her garden was well tended, she followed the path between her garden and the Big House. It led under a shade tree at the end of three rows of lesser houses. Each of the lesser houses was progressively smaller until the most recent construction which was no larger than the Big House's pantry.

The silent streets between the buildings were neatly kept—Ben trundled up and down them an hour a day when he was at the Homestead, his horse hooves clop-clopping while his wheels clattered behind. The dirt of the streets was well packed. The grass along them perfectly trimmed. Bright flowers lined the walkways.

The houses themselves were mismatched prefab panels as carefully puzzled into place as possible. At Mary's insistence, they had been painted brilliant hues. The result was a second garden of sorts, though she had never thought of it as such.

The cleaner-bots were performing the morning dusting. Mary entered the first house where the low-riding, sinuous, cleaning bots utilized their multiple attachments in vacuuming the floors and washing the windows while moving the box furniture around and wiping it down. They paused their tasks to hover over and bump gently against her legs. She checked their readouts, confirming all systems were functioning normal, and patted them in turn. "Good job, fellas."

The sound of their vacuums resumed as she left them to their work.

Between the first row of rainbow-splashed dwellings and the Big House was an open yard. The repair kiosk sat in the center, a rectangular stela central to the mechanicals' daily routine and inscribed with the words, "Care. Obey. Protect."

Powerbays ringed the kiosk. Tall, semi-circular protective walls of gray plazsteel, the bays contained an array of power sockets and diagnostic processes set around a cradle. Once shiny and the newest accessory for all mechanicals large or small, they had been patched and repaired over the years.

She stopped beside the largest one and felt a subroutine kick in. Worry. The programed "ticks" began in a choreographed sequence. Sad eyes. Biting of the lip. Sigh Number Eight. A gentle palm pressed against the bay.

Ben had been gone too long. If the Appaloosa Spot Solar Cells had malfunctioned, he would be trapped. But he kept a careful watch over them. What else could keep him? Unless…?

Hope routine balancing out the worry, she passed among the bays and climbed the steps to the wide, wraparound porch of the Big House—the original building placed on the Homestead long ago. Before her time, certainly. Clem and Doc, though, they'd been here from the beginning.

She entered the large white house via the side door and into the mudroom where a line of knee-high boots waited under a bright blue painted bench. Cleaned and polished, the boots were ready for their owners, for human feet to be shoved into them. They were ready for the joy of mud and grass stains gathered in the fields.

The worry threatened to unbalance her again, but she clung desperately to hope. Those boots would know the smell of human feet. They would make a happy, terrible clomping across the porch and down the steps. And all would be right in the world.

Retrieving the cleaning supplies from the cupboards above the inactive laundry bots, she set about making the surfaces shine. Housekeeping was a subroutine of her child minder protocol and she had supplemented her own knowledge with the cleanerbots programing. Working at double speed, she cleaned the Big House in record time. It's twelve bedrooms, formal sitting room, education slash game room, medical bay and den. All of it sparkled and shone when she was finished.

Her eye fell out a few times. Grumbling, she paused each time to settle it into its socket.

In the big kitchen with the large windows and even larger counter spaces, she used the flour that Clem had ground from the grain he had planted, tended, and harvested. She mixed it with the eggs from the chickens and the milk from the cows to make bread dough. Humming a song, Lullaby Number Twenty-eight, she kneaded the dough.

Push. Push. Push. Flip. Pat. Push. Push. Push. Flip. Pat-pat.

The softy floury dough felt almost like the jell-bear. Almost.... If she gathered it like this and this, and wrapped it in a flour sack towel, it almost felt like an infant in her arms. She poked small holes in the top of the unbaked loaf peeking out of the towel. Two holes side by side with a curved line beneath them.

Inside of her, programming collided, protocols crisscrossing. The urge to take the infant to the nursery juxtaposed against the baker routine, the need to set the loaf in a pan on the warm and let it rise. Let it grow. Let it become what it was meant to be.

It was with great effort that the baker routine won against the primary function of child minder.

Mary was quiet as she gathered with the others on the porch at midday. It was unnecessary, they could have worked until their power cells ran down, but they gathered, nonetheless, in imitation of their makers. It was a vigil they kept. A service observed.

Spider clattered up, waving a forelimb. Half as tall as Mary, domed Spider had spider-leg shaped attachments that made him quite useful on the homestead, and the chickens and cows were happy and well-tended animals thanks to him. When he stopped waving the attachment, she saw a wire had gotten caught in the pinchers. She carefully unwound it.

"Mary, Mary," Clem said as he climbed up the stairs. "Mother Mary full of grace, you have flour on your face."

He could not know how his words drilled into her minder protocol. How they mocked her incomplete equations. She looked away and wiped the flour off her face, wishing it were tears. Did not tears ease the pressure of a human's unfulfilled programming?

A Most Unusual Garden

"Mary, are you wearing pink #ef75cb?" Doc asked as he joined them. He was a tubular bot with a variety of appendages that assisted him in his daily routines. His primary function was data collection: weather patterns, soil composition, market trends, animal genetics, familial history, and the like.

"I mixed it myself," Mary said unable to prevent herself from touching the paint she'd applied to her casing in a cardigan pattern the night before.

"It suits you," Doc declared and turned his tin can head to Clem.

Clem was silent. He watched the two cleaner bots hover over the wood planks of the porch.

They were all silent and Mary did not like the silence today. It was too loud. Too heavy. Too ripe.

"I'm going to feed the ducks." She walked into the house, hip servo protesting. Picking up the three-day-old loaves of bread, she carried them out to the pond.

It was a lovely pond that lay west of the big house and among weeping willows. Bright grasses grew around it and water lilies on it. Large orange and red fish swam gracefully among the lily roots.

Blue and white Buckbills and iridescent Greenspots quacked at her, telling her to hurry and break the bread. As fast as she sprinkled the pieces on the ground, the ducks snatched them up, too hurried to enjoy their afternoon communion.

She watched the ripples on the pond as the ducks returned to their swimming. They quacked their ducky gossip as they did so. Did they share information about the bread?

"It was tastier yesterday than today."

"Well, my good friend, I thought today's crumbs superior."

Those musings led her to write a children's story and compose a haiku. She wandered back to her garden and recited both story and poem to her plantlings. One of the dolls blinked and smiled while the dogbot wagged its tail.

"Mah-mah..." Dolly Wolly said in a rundown voice.

"No mamas here," Mary said, patting the doll on its head. "But I would appreciate it if you would grow one for me."

Her attempts to convince the biopanels to take root and grow something—anything—were interrupted by a great clattering. She looked up and her happiness routines kicked in. A smile spread across her face.

Ben had returned.

Anticipation routine joined happiness and she was practically dizzy with them as she went to meet the centaurdroid. He was tall, broad-shouldered, plain yet angular. Blue humanoid body merged seamlessly with a darker blue equine body. A full and overflowing wagon was hitched to him and it rattled in behind as his steel hooves clattered up the road.

One of Spider's small satellite bots, one they called Web, road on Ben's shoulder. As Ben brought the wagon to a standstill in its parking place, Web scurried down the centaurdroid's back, around the Appaloosa Solar Power Cells, and began releasing the harness.

"Welcome back, Ben."

"Mary. It's good to be home." Ben's right rear hoof stomped the ground for emphasis before he walked out of the unfastened harness.

A Most Unusual Garden

"How was your journey?" An eagerness filled her voice that was hard to miss.

"It went well." His voice was deep and rumbled like timpani.

"Excellent! You found a box of reverse coils," Doc said as he approached the cart, eagerly taking inventory.

"Two," Ben said. He lifted the items off the top of the wagon.

Spider came along and joined them as they unloaded what Ben had scavenged. Prefab sheets and repair bars and bio filament. As they worked, Mary cast many glances at Ben, hoping to read something in his movements.

When they were half-finished, Doc plugged into Ben's data system and processed the information there. "The solar cells were ninety-three percent efficient. That is good."

"Yes," agreed Ben as they continued unloading. The second half of the cart was mostly building and repair materials. They were, after all, preparing for the return of five adult generations of Homesteaders.

Clem didn't come up from the fields until they were almost finished. By then, the afternoon sky was shading to a pinkish red.

It was then Ben gave the answer to the question that had been trying to escape Mary's vocal processor since she'd greeted him. An answer he wouldn't give until they were all together. It was one, simple, solitary word.

"No."

In Ben's deep, rolling voice, it carried a weight of finality that Mary could not accept. "No!? Not ... anyone? Anything?"

"No."

Clem said nothing. He opened the repair kiosk with his skin-soft hand and withdrew a honer, running it over the edge of his scythe.

Ben gave Mary a sad shake of his head and finished removing the last prefab panel from the wagon.

Doc said, "There are forty-two settlements of substantial size remaining on planet. Ben's solar cells make it possible to visit each one."

He said this as if the words would trigger Mary's happiness routine. She didn't know what to say, so she applied a patchkit to a gouge she had noticed on Web's dome.

"It won't matter," Clem said, putting the honer away and swinging his scythe-hand back into its compartment. "No one will be there."

"They will!" The words felt hot and bitter in Mary's vocal processor. "They are out there Clem! And they are coming back!"

She walked away. If she were human, she would be crying. What did that feel like—warm liquid salt running down skin-soft cheeks? She knew what it was like to wipe tears away. To comfort a sniffling child. To "make things better." It had been too long, far too long, since she had done so. Her subroutines ached with the need of fulfillment.

She heard him coming. His footsteps carrying him through the sunset-touched garden. She was on the verge of telling him to go away when he thrust an object into her field of vision.

"Ben brought you this."

Half soft-bot, half jell, the octopus weakly waved one of its limbs while its overly large eyes blinked slowly open and closed. It made a squishy sound when she closed her hand around it.

"Easy, now, sweetie," Mary crooned to ... her. It was a "her". "You're safe. You'll never be alone."

Cradling the octopus in her arms, she rocked back and forth until the programming in the little thing's soft-bot routine settled, until the jell with its biogel basis ceased reaching out for comfort.

Humans had made them. The one-eyed dogbots, and Mary, and the jell-bears, and Clem, and everyone. They'd made them in their own image, with the ability for laughter and happiness routines and a biologically coded need for contact, for community.

And, then, their Makers had abandoned the Homestead. Apparently, they had abandoned the planet, too. Not even Doc or Clem knew why.

But the humans were out there, somewhere, and they were coming back. They were!

Still cradling the octopus, she looked up at the evening star shining through the golden-orange clouds floating across the twilight blue. She wondered if, at that moment, their Makers were flying between the stars in silver ships? Were they racing home? Dreaming of their fields and the pond and the Big House?

"Have you ever thought," Clem said softly in his farmhand voice. "They need not return because they never truly left? They are within us, Mary. Thought patterns and emotional subroutines. You are Mary. I am Clem. Long ago, the human Mary and Clem, built this place.

"When they needed help, they programmed us in their image, to live the rhythms of their lives with them. Eventually, when they went away, their hearts remained. The parts of them that mattered most. They will never be lost, Mary. They live on. In us."

He scruffed at the ground with his metal boot like human Clem once scruffed at the ground with his heavy work shoe. "Mary had a flock of lambs, their souls as cold as snow, but Mary's tender, minding care the lambs were sure to show."

There was a pause, the space of a human exhalation. "You tend us well, Mary."

His arm whirled, the spade hand spinning out to replace the skin-soft hand. He dug a hole for the octopus not far from the jell-bear.

Mary's head jerked as she tried to process Clem's words. The motion caused her eye to fall out. It dangled on its coil, and a trickle of warm oil escaped the corner of the socket, rolling down her skin-soft cheek.

"Mary, Mary, don't cry, Mary," Clem said, catching her eye with one hand and wiping the streak of oil away with a dusty thumb. He used a tool in his finger compartment to scratch at the grooves on the ocular piece, deepening them a shade. Gently, he set her eye in place. This time, the grooves caught and held.

They watched the last of the day, the last visual note of the sun echo golden across the landscape. They sensed the same within themselves. The final measures of a song echoing on.

ABOUT THE AUTHORS

TRACY EIRE has been a professional writer for almost a decade writing to a variety of needs, from the magazine Beautiful Bizarre, to collaborations with artists like Jenny Boot. In the mid-2000s, she started her art career and fiction publications. An oil painter with interest in watercolour painting, she was creatively influenced by her childhood home of Newfoundland. The wildness, mysticism, and kindness of this Northern island home just a step out of time, translated into optimism and depictions of light in art. The stamp of those wild climes and pagan survivals became strong impulses in her writing. They can be seen from her rich cast of mystical characters, to the haunting moments we all experience to one side of the flow of normal life, captured in her books. A seasoned writer, she's neurodiverse. Overcoming her disabilities with grit and flexibility creates a highly individual point of view in her work.

Please visit her at <u>tracyeire.site</u>

N.D. GRAY once dreamed of being an astronaut. Now, she writes about characters who reach for the stars, and fills their stories with magic, mayhem, and moonlight.

When she's not writing, she works full time as a caregiver specializing in adults with I/DD, hangs out with the pup pack, and enjoys several creative pursuits, including acrylic painting.

Please visit her at ndgray.com

ELIZABETH KNOLLSTON has always been an avid reader of science fiction and fantasy. Now she works on turning her vivid imagination of alien worlds, long lost secrets of the universe, mystical realms and the obligatory dragon into stories of her own. Often blending religious questions and an abiding love for archeology into the driving forces behind her worlds. When not daydreaming about why the local pet store doesn't carry baby dragons, or being a part of a manned mission to Mars, Elizabeth teaches therapeutic riding, spends time with her dog, works in the garden, and loves giving back to the community.

HEIDI MOONE writes things. She says, "I've started to publish some of these things to share them with others. I like writing stories about fantastic places and the magic in the everyday world. I've been reading, and writing, from an early age, and I come from a tradition of oral storytellers, in rural Newfoundland. I love the written word, and it's my favorite medium to communicate my ideas to anyone looking for a new world to explore, and new people to meet along the way."

Please visit her at **heidimoone.com**

KARLI STITES is a tech nerd by day (and also by night). Faced with an overload of creativity that had nowhere to go, she started writing sci-fi and fantasy novels. Karli published the first book in her debut series in 2019, and her young adult romance space opera trilogy, Synchrony Souls, will be completed soon. A lover of all things fantasy and mythological, she recently embarked on a new writing journey, diving into a dragon world full of mystery and magic. The first book in her fantasy dragon shifter series, *Rise of the Drakoni,* will release at the end of 2021.

Find out more about her current books and keep up to date on her upcoming releases at **karlistitesauthor.com.**

thank
you
for
reading